DEAR

SERENITY,

BLAZE

SOUL Publications

D1416565

Dear Serenity: The Letter Chronicles   Blaze

SOUL Publications

Chapter 1

Waking up Serenity frowned up her face hating to move out her warm cozy bed. But she had to get up and get ready for work and get her son Kian ready for his first day of school. Glancing over her shoulder she watched her husband Aaron as he peacefully slept. She leaned over and kissed his lips.

"Yo, chill with that," Aaron grumpily said, pushing her away.

"Ugh, what the fuck is wrong with you? When has it been a problem to kiss you in the morning?"

"That shit gets aggravating, especially when I don't have to get up this damn early. You don't see me bothering you when I get up early and you don't, do you?"

Serenity sucked her teeth. "Whatever Aaron." She got out the bed and grabbed her robe. She looked back at her husband wanting to say something, but she wasn't in the mood for the back and forth with him. As she walked down the hall she could hear her son yelling. All she could do is shake her head knowing his ass was playing his game instead of getting ready for school. Opening his door, what she already knew was confirmed.

"Boy, if you don't get off that damn game and get ready for school," Serenity fussed, placing her hands on her hips.

"Ok mom, just five more minutes," Kian begged, never taking his eyes off the television screen.

Serenity wasn't having it. She walked into his room and hit the power button on his Xbox one.

"Nooo," Kian cried out. "Ma, I was almost done."

"Get your little ass up and get ready for school."

Kian slammed his controller down and sucked his teeth while mumbling something under his breath. At the age of twelve he had a temper and many times Serenity had to check him.

"What was that?" Serenity challenged him to repeat.

Kian turned around with a fake smile plastered on his face. "I love you?"

"Umm hmm," Serenity chuckled.

"Ma, is dad still here?"

"Yea, he's sleeping. What's wrong?"

"Nothing, just need to make sure he will still be here to take me to football practice after school."

"I'm sure he will be baby. This your first year playing and he wouldn't miss it." Serenity said, trying to convince herself as well as Kian. "Now, hurry up. I will go fix you something to eat."

Serenity headed downstairs and started a breakfast for Kian. She quickly fixed Kian some pancakes, eggs and bacon before heading back to her room to get ready for work. When she entered her bedroom, she got this eerie feeling hearing Aaron on the phone inside the bathroom. She tried to ease inside without being heard, but Kian came rushing in the room.

"Dad," Kian yelled coming in.

Next Serenity heard Aaron telling the person he would call them back before he stepped out the bathroom. She looked at Aaron warily when he walked into the bedroom.

"What's up Ki?" Aaron asked, tossing his phone back on the bed.

"Are you still taking me to practice after school?" Kian questioned.

"Yea, daddy got you." Aaron smiled. "Now go eat so your little ass can get to school. Damn, my boy in the sixth grade already." Aaron smiled.

The whole time Serenity's eyes was glued to Aaron's phone, wondering who he was on the phone with this early in the morning. Once Kian left the room, she asked.

"Who was you talking to?"

"What are you talking about?" Aaron played dumb.

"Just now, on the phone. Who was you talking to?"

"Oh, that was James. He said he needs my help with something at the office, so I'm going in after all." Aaron quickly answered.

"Oh." Was all Serenity could muster up and say. She didn't want to believe the thoughts that was running wild in her head, but she couldn't help herself. Not dwelling on the issues too long, she got herself ready for work. She could have been a stay at home mom, she did it for a while but got bored. So, for the past year she worked at the bank as a teller.

"Aaron, please don't forget about today. Do I need to call and remind you?"

"Do I look like a fucking child? I'm not going to forget!"

"I was just asking because you know how you get caught up with your damn work. Especially now with the promotion, it seems like they put more on you. But excuse the fuck out of me for trying to be a fucking wife."

"Yea well, you can be my wife without the damn nagging." Aaron hissed.

"Oh, so I'm a nag now?" Serenity asked, getting up in his face.

"Ren, back up man."

"Answer my damn question?"

"Look, I'm not in the mood to talk about this. We both need to get out of here and to work." Aaron kissed her cheek and started taking off his clothes to take a shower. "Ren, can you please iron my shirt?"

"Oh, now you want the nagging wife to do something. Nah, your hands not broke, do it yourself." Serenity hissed, pushing Aaron out her way and going into the bathroom.

"Hold up, what you doing? I already had the shower started for..." Aaron started to say.

"Yea, well, like you said, I need to get ready for work." Serenity smugly smiled, walking into the bathroom and slamming the door.

"Man, you petty as hell Serenity." Aaron fussed.

"Yep," Serenity replied on the other side of the door. She hurried and took her shower, so she could get out the door and to work on time.

****

It seems as if the day was dragging by and Serenity was ready to get off of work. It was her lunch break and she walked into the break room, joining her coworker Treasure. They both started working at the bank at the same time and became good friends over the year. Treasure glanced up from her phone seeing Serenity coming in.

"Why the long face boo?" Treasure asked.

"Girl, I am so ready to get out of here," Serenity complained sitting down at the table.

"That makes two of us." Treasure agreed. Looking back at her phone, Treasure loudly yelled, "What the fuck."

"What happened?" Serenity's head quickly popped up looking over at Treasure.

"I'm checking my child support to see if jackass' payment posted yet and this shit says twenty-five dollars was deposited."

"Twenty-five," Serenity mocked with a slight snicker. "Now Junior should be ashamed of himself. What the hell is that going to help you with. I know something is better than nothing , but damn twenty-five whole dollars?"

"Ugh, mind you, this shit supposed to come out his damn check. I see I have to call my damn caseworker later." Treasure shook her head in disgust. Her son's father did the bare minimum for her ten-year-old son. Normally she didn't bother him about his child support payment and took what she could get, but twenty-five dollars was where she was drawing the line.

The security guard that was on shift heard Treasure and added his two cents to what Treasure told Serenity, "That's what you get for not letting me play step daddy. I could finance more than twenty-five damn dollars and some good wood." He winked at her.

"Shut up Lamont and mind your damn business." Treasure hissed.

"Treasure, you did play Lamont and I'm sure he could do better than Junior." Serenity commented, sharing a laugh with Lamont.

"See, Serenity knows what time it is." Lamont said, giving Treasure a wink.

Treasure put up her middle finger, ignoring both Lamont and Serenity.

"So Lamont, did they hire somebody else to take Chris' spot? I hate working with old man Roger. His old ass be flirting, and I am sick of his dirty jokes. I'm going to report his ass for sexual harassment." Serenity stated.

"Pump your brakes before you get the old man fired," Lamont laughed. "But yea, my old college roommate got the job. He just moved back to Philly."

"Lawd, that means he's an ain't shit nigga just like you." Treasure stated, rolling her eyes.

"Just like your baby father," Lamont shot back. "I'm going to make my rounds." Lamont gave Treasure a scowl before walking away.

Serenity made sure Lamont was out of earshot before she said something to Treasure. She nudged her with her elbow. "Why you be doing him like that?"

"Girl please, Lamont is just like the rest of these lames. He just looking to fuck and I don't have time for that shit." Treasure looked around, then leaned closer to Serenity. "You know I caught him the other day coming out of the back room with Ronda. Then, his ass had some nerve to ask me out like he wasn't in the room fucking that girl."

"You sound jealous," Serenity teased.

Treasure sucked her teeth. "Jealous of what, that? Hell no. I'm just sick of these men playing games. I wish I had me an Aaron at home," Treasure said, referring to Serenity's husband.

Serenity let out a snicker. Little did Treasure know, Aaron wasn't what she wanted either. From the outside looking in people would think she had the perfect life. It was just the opposite but she put up the perfect front. She and Aaron met freshman year of college and been together since. As of lately, she feels her marriage has been falling apart. She tried her best to make her marriage work, but Aaron wasn't making it easy for her. She knew her son shouldn't be the reason she stayed in a unhealthy marriage, but she was trying to live by her vows, for better or worse.

"Serenity," Treasure yelled, getting her attention.

Serenity shook her head, snapping out of her daze. "Yea."

"Girl you ok, I lost you for a second? What's on your mind?" Treasure questioned.

"I'm good. Let me go use the restroom before I go back out there." Serenity quickly got up from her chair and went to the bathroom. She was on the verge of tears thinking about her husband. She didn't have the proof, but she got an eerie feeling he was cheating on her. His actions say it, but she didn't know for sure and it was stressing her out, worrying herself over it.

Once Serenity used the restroom she went back to her station and watched the clock like hawk, wishing it would hurry up and strike 5 p.m. She was more than ready to get off. The rest of the day seemed to drag and it wasn't much work Serenity had to do. So using some of her time, she was thinking about ways to spice up her marriage and getting it back on track like it should be.

"Hey, didn't you say Aaron was taking Kian to football practice or whatever today? You want to hit up happy hour?" Treasure asked. "My brother got Justice for me and I can use a few drinks."

"Yea, I guess I can use a few drinks too . I have to go home first and make sure Kian's things are out. I don't trust him or Aaron to have everything." Serenity laughed.

"Ok, I can meet you at the bar." Treasure happily said.

Finally, they were free from the work day. Serenity hurried home to get Kian's football gear out. She was glad Treasure invited her out to have a few drinks because she needed to clear her head. Unfortunately, she had other things to deal with when she got home. Pulling into her driveway, she saw Aaron was walking out the house with a few bags in his hands. She got out her car and stood there for second watching Aaron, waiting for him to acknowledge her. When he didn't, she let out a sigh.

"Where are you going?" She asked, breaking her silence.

"If you see me putting bags in my car, where do you think I'm going Serenity?" Aaron snarled.

Serenity closed her eyes and let out a heavy sigh. In her mind she was choking the shit out of Aaron for his smart mouth. Taking a deep breath, she counted to ten. Once she was done she opened her eyes and blankly stared at her Aaron with the urge to smack his ass. This wasn't the man she married. This wasn't the man she fell in love with. Something definitely was going on and she hated the distance that has grown between them.

Letting out another sigh she said, "Don't be a smartass Aaron. I see you're putting bags in the damn car meaning you're going on a business trip, but where to Jackass?"

"You better watch your damn mouth. I'm going New York. James needs my help and we can't afford to lose this client he's trying to get." Aaron explained.

"Really? So you're putting Kian on the back burner for something that don't concern you?"

"What the fuck you mean it don't concern me? Serenity, who does James work for? His problems are my problems." Aaron hissed.

"For how long?"

"Why?" He asked getting irritated with all the questions.

"Because I want to fucking know, that's why. When has it been a problem for me to ask my husband how long he's going to be gone? Need I remind you, you've broken another promise you made to your son.

He was so excited about you taking him to football practice."

Aaron quickly tossed his bags in the car and stood in front of Serenity. He narrowed his eyes and clenched his jaws. "You like this house we live in, right? You love that damn car you're fucking driving, right?" Serenity didn't answer him and he got loud. "Right!"

"What's your fucking point Aaron," Serenity scoffed.

Aaron let out a chuckle. "If I don't help my brother close this deal the company will miss out on money, and that's money I will miss out on. Therefore, I need to do whatever it takes to make sure that happens. That's my damn point."

"So, basically you're saying fuck me and Kian?"

Aaron ran his hands over his face letting out a sigh. "Ugh, you know that's not what I am saying. Listen, it's just a damn practice. Ki understands daddy gotta go to work. Now, I need to go to the airport and he's in there waiting for you to take him."

"Really! This the type of bullshit..." Serenity started to say but stopped when she saw Kian standing at the door. She threw her hands up and just left it alone. She texted Treasure telling her she couldn't make it. Just as she was stuffing her hands in her pocket, her phone was ringing. She let out a sigh answering Treasure's call.

"Why, what happened. Ugh, you was so hype to go out." Treasure whined in the phone.

"Girl, as much as I want to come out because Lord knows I can use the drinks, I have to take Kian to the field. Aaron have to go out of town for work."

"Ok. Ugh, I really don't want to go solo, but I understand. See you tomorrow."

Ending her call, Serenity placed her phone in her back pocket. Kian looked up at her with the saddest set of eyes she had ever seen. It killed her seeing his little face filled with sadness.

"He always does this," Kian angrily said and stomped upstairs to his room.

"Ki," Serenity called out to him and followed him to his room. "Kian, baby, you know your father..."

"Mom, stop. You don't have to lie for him." Kian said, cutting her off. "I'm twelve years old and not a little kid that don't understand. Daddy always working but you work and are always here for me, so why he can't do the same?"

Again, Serenity was speechless. Kian stunned her into silence, calling Aaron out on his bullshit.

"Why he just doesn't leave." Kian blurted out.

"Because we're a family. Why would you say that Kian?"

"Because he's always gone. It's not the same anymore."

Just hearing Kian's little voice speaking the truth broke Serenity's heart. She didn't realize that Kian was paying attention to Aaron's actions just as she was.

"So, I guess I can't play football now?" Kian crossed his arms over his chest and kicked at the air.

"No baby, you can. I'm about to change clothes so I can take you." Serenity said with a half-smile."

"But you had plans to go out." Kian pointed out.

"You don't worry about me, ok. I got you."

Kian nodded his head. "Ok." He lowered his head and pouted all the way to his room. When he walked in, he saw his phone going off on the bed. He picked it up and read the text from his friend Mykel. Once he was finish reading it, he ran down to his mother's room.

"Mom, Mykel just texted and asked if I wanted to ride to practice with him and his dad. His dad is one of the coaches."

Serenity sat silent for a second, giving it some thought.

"Please mom? You can go out now," Kian pleaded.

Letting out a sigh, Serenity gave in. "Ok Kian."

He ran over to her and kissed her cheek. "Thanks mom."

"I will come pick you up. And after that, we can go grab something to eat."

"Ok." Kian kissed her cheek again and ran out the room to get his things."

Soon as Serenity got downstairs there was knock at her front door. When she opened it she was stunned into silence, eyeing the fine man standing in front of her. His honey colored skin was shining with the help of the sun beating down on him. His hair was freshly cut and his waves was on point. He had the prettiest set of eyes and kissable lips. He was about 6 feet tall and had an athletic build. She couldn't help herself when her eyes traveled further down, checking out what was under his basketball shorts. After sneaking a peep she raised her eyes and looked him in the face. Getting a better glimpse at him, Serenity thought he may have been somebody she knew. She then tilted her head and squinted her eyes. Once recognition set in her hands flew to her mouth.

"Oh my God, Markieff," she called out his name for clarification.

Markieff stepped back to get a better look at Serenity. His eyes widened once he realized who this stranger was calling his name.

"Well, I be damn. Serenity Beal. Don't just stand there, give your boy some damn love," he said with his arms wide opened.

Serenity wrapped her arms around him and hugged him. His cologne invaded her nostrils and she was alarmed about what happened next. She felt the heat growing between her legs and quickly stepped out of Markieff's embrace. She shyly looked down tucking her hair behind her ear.

"Wow, you all grown up girl." Markieff said, giving her a once over liking what he was seeing. The last time he saw Serenity she was a skinny seventeen-year-old. Now she was a grown woman with all the right curves. "Umm," Markieff said to himself. After checking her out, he looked up and asked, "So, how's the family doing?"

"Everybody's good. Oh my God, my dad is going to be too hype when I tell him I saw you."

"Yea, I need to link up with the old man. Definitely would love to catch up with him. Damn, I can't believe I'm standing in front of Serenity Beal." Markieff said, admiring her again.

"It's Serenity Porter now."

Markieff's eyes quickly lowered to her hand checking her ring finger. "Lucky man."

"I guess," Serenity dryly answered. She then pushed Markieff back getting a better look at him. "Looking good Scooter." She complimented him, calling him by his nickname.

"Shhh, don't be calling me that out loud."

"Boy hush." She said, playfully hitting his arm.

Moments later, Kian came running down the stairs and ran out the door.

"Thank you for picking him up. I will come get him once y'all are done." Serenity said.

"Nah, I can bring him home. After practice I was thinking about taking them to get something to eat, unless you trying to feed me tonight?"

Serenity playfully hit Markieff. "You are still a mess. Well, I guess since I don't have to take him to the field, I can whip something up for you big head."

"Dad, come on we late. I'm ready to play ball," Mykel yelled from the car.

Markieff snickered. "I guess that's my cue to go. I was just fucking with you. You don't have to cook. I will grab something on the way, you need me to pick you up something?"

"No, I'm good." Serenity smiled.

Markieff backpedaled, walking off the porch shaking his head. "Damn, you're looking good Lucky Charm." He winked before turning around doing a slight jog to his car.

Serenity couldn't help but blush. It's been years since she was drawn to any man other than her husband. But then again, Markieff wasn't any other man to her. She couldn't help but run her tongue across her lips as she watched Markieff get into the car. When he looked towards the house, she quickly shut the door.

"Lawd, Markieff is still fine," she said out loud, resting her back against the door.

Once upon a time, those two were inseparable. They lived next door from each other from the ages of five to seventeen. Markieff's family moved away and of course, they lost all contact. Markieff was like the son her father never had, but she didn't look at him like a brother. Although Markieff's father was in the picture, he was always away for work. Markieff spent most of his time at Serenity's house helping her father. Benny, Serenity's father owned a few barber shops and other businesses in Philly. Benny always had Markieff tagging along while he went to work. Markieff helped around the shop amongst other things Benny needed to do, legal and illegal. Benny also was a bookie and sometimes Markieff went to pick up money for him from people. Overall, Benny always treated Markieff as if he was his own son.

Picking up her phone she called her father to tell him the good news. She knew he was going to be hype to hear Markieff was back. As she waited for her dad to answer the phone, she couldn't contain the wide smile that painted her face.

"Hey baby girl," Benny answered the phone.

"Dad, guess who is back in Philly."

"Shit, must be Obama the way you're smiling on the damn phone." Benny joked.

"No fool. But, Markieff."

"Oh really. Where did you see my boy at? I haven't seen him since they moved."

"He just left my house. He is one of the football coaches and picked Kian up."

"I see. But why isn't Aaron taking him to practice?" Benny angrily questioned.

Serenity let out a sigh. "He had a business trip that popped up."

"Where?"

"New York."

"I see. Well, I'm glad Markieff looking out. Wait, how the hell he know where you live?"

"His son is Mykel, Kian's little friend."

"I knew it was a reason I liked that kid. Listen when you see him again, make sure you call me. I would love to talk to him. And, I will be having a talk with Aaron's ass. I don't say much, but I see. Since he got this little promotion, his ass been Casper the friendly ghost and that's not cool."

"Damn, even my father sees the bullshit," Serenity thought to herself. "Daddy don't worry about that. I will talk to Aaron."

"You sure, because you know I don't play about mine," Benny reminded her.

"Yes, I'm sure daddy," Serenity laughed.

"Ok. Love you baby and don't forget to have Markieff call me."

"I will." Serenity ended her call and realized that she was still smiling from ear to ear since Markieff left. "No Serenity," she said to herself, shaking off the thoughts she was having.

She picked up her phone and texted Aaron. It was just a simple I love and miss you. She told him they needed to sit down and talk once he got home. Hearing Kian's cries of Aaron not being home didn't sit too well with her and it was time to get her house back in order.

Chapter 2

"Wifey said she loves and misses you," Aaron's side piece said, reading Serenity's text message.

Aaron rushed out the bathroom and snatched the phone from her hands. "What the fuck I tell you about touching my shit, Nene," he snarled.

Nene sucked her teeth. "Boy please. You know how many times I text her, pretending to be you."

"You petty man," Aaron laughed. He plopped down on the bed, picking up his phone and dialed Serenity's number. He let out a sigh, waiting for her to answer. It rung a few times and went to her voicemail. Pulling the phone from his ear, he blankly stared at it because that wasn't like Serenity not to answer. Then he remembered about football and figured she didn't hear her phone.

"So, how much more time do I have to wait for you to leave her?" Nene questioned.

Aaron clenched his jaws and slowly turned to face Nene. "Look, don't be nagging me about that shit. I thought I came over here to fucking relax. If I wanted to hear that nagging shit, I would have stayed home with my wife." He shook his head.

"Really? So, I'm a nag because I want to know when you're going to stop playing and leave somebody you sit up and complain to me about? You even said you don't love her like you used to, so why are you staying? And don't even sit here and tell me that bullshit about it's for Kian. You can still be a father to him."

"Ugh," Aaron grunted. "I know that, but it's not that easy." Aaron slid over and wrapped his arms around Nene's waist, pulling her closer to him. He then placed a soft kiss on her neck. "You know I love you and I just need a little more time. But let's be real about this shit. If you wouldn't have been so stubborn back then you would be wifey, not her." He then stuck his hands down her pants, and with his thumb he rubbed her love button.

"Stop," Nene tried to push him away.

Stubbornly ignoring her, Aaron got down on the floor and pulled her pants down with him. He looked up at her with a smirk on his face as he buried his head between her legs. Nene let out a loud moan as his wet tongue connected with her warm center.

"I hate you," Nene moaned.

"I know you do baby. I promise, soon I will be all yours." Aaron sucked hard on her clit, causing her to let out a loud scream. "Umm hmm, let that shit out," he said between slurps. He moved his head in a perfect rhythm as he feasted on her pussy. It wasn't long before Nene was leaking all her juices inside his mouth. Aaron took his time and licked her dry before coming up for air. He stood to his feet and dropped his pants releasing his erect dick.

"He said it's his turn," Aaron laughed, pointing down to his dick.

Nene chuckled and as hard as she could, she smacked his dick and stood to her feet. "You won't be fucking shit until you leave her. I am sick of playing second to this bitch. So until then, don't fucking call me and you better hope no other nigga comes and..."

"Man, kill that noise. If your ass wanted somebody else, you would have been bounced. So stop playing." Aaron hissed walking closer. Nene pushed him back and he gave her a scowl. "You're for real?"

"As real as it gets. I am not doing this shit with you. I been playing the sideline too fucking long. This on and off shit needs to stop. Unless you're about to get on your phone and tell Serenity it's over, you can kiss my ass."

"You fucking up our night over some bullshit? I put my son on the back burner to come over here with your ass and this what you do? Man, fuck you. This shit over. I don't even know why I stayed this long with your ass. Ungrateful ass bitch," Aaron hissed. He got up and started packing his bag, still mumbling under his breath. He could feel Nene's eyes on him. He stopped what he was doing and looked up at her.

"Did you just call me a bitch?" Nene questioned for clarification.

"I didn't stutter."

Nene let out a snicker. She got in his face and smacked him hard across the face. Out of reflex Aaron did the same, shocking the hell out of Nene.

"Yo, keep your fucking hands to yourself," Aaron warned her.

"You know you fucked up right?"

"What the fuck you going to do? Get somebody to beat my ass? Yea, go ahead and see what the fuck happens to your ass."

"Get out my fucking house Aaron." Nene pointed towards the door.

"I'm going. And don't fucking call me for no dick when your ass realizes you fucked up a good thing."

"Nigga, you're not the only sucker I been fucking," Nene taunted.

"I knew I shouldn't have fucked with your hoe ass. Don't fucking call me for shit." Taking out his wallet, he peeled four hundred-dollar bills from his money clip. "You know what the money for."

"Aww, you salty nigga? You in your feelings because you thought I was a dumb hoe and was only fucking you? Sorry boo, but you weren't. And the money you continue to kick out goes on my nigga's books." Nene was lying, but Aaron didn't know that. She was just pissed and wanted to hurt Aaron. She doesn't know why she's so in love with him, but she was and it was killing her that he wasn't hers.

As much as Aaron wanted to put hands on Nene, he wasn't trying to take a chance of her calling the police. He wouldn't have been able to explain to Serenity how he ended up in the city jail when he was supposed to be in New York. His jaws clenched, badly wanting to wrap his hands around Nene's neck.

****

Serenity had just stepped out the shower when she heard the doorbell going off. She quickly put on a pair of pants and t-shirts then rushed downstairs. When she opened it, she found Markieff standing there smiling from ear to ear.

"Honey, we home." Markieff joked with his arms opened wide.

"Nigga, you're not home." Serenity laughed.

"Ard, ard, you got that one."

Kian came running up the steps and was all smiles. "Ma, I didn't know you and Kel's daddy grew up together. He said you was his best friend. That's decent because me and Mykel best friends."

"Yes baby, me and Markieff grew up together." Serenity smiled.

"I'm going to wash. Thank you Uncle Markieff for taking me to practice today." Kian said then ran off to his room.

"Wow, you told him to call you Uncle?" Serenity giggled.

Markieff shrugged his shoulders. "Yea, why not."

"I didn't say he couldn't."

Markieff bit down on his bottom lip, lustfully eyeing Serenity. They stood there in an awkward silence. Serenity wanted to turn away to avoid the intense stare, but couldn't pull her eyes from his face. Before either one could say anything Aaron's car was pulling into the driveway.

"Who the fuck is that?" Markieff asked, getting into protective mode.

"Ugh, look at you being nosey as hell. That would be my husband."

"Oh ok. I thought Kian said he went away for work? That's why I was asking."

"Yea, I thought so too." Serenity said to herself.

Aaron spotted Markieff standing on the porch with Serenity and quickly got out the car. He walked up the steps never taking his eyes off Serenity. Getting up in her face he clenched his jaws giving her a death stare.

"Who the fuck is this nigga standing on my porch?" Aaron snarled as his tall frame towered over Serenity.

Serenity opened her mouth to answer Aaron, but Markieff quickly stepped in putting some space between the two. He moved Serenity out the way and answered the question.

"I'm Markieff, a friend of the family and your son's football coach." He said, extending his hand trying to be peaceful.

Aaron kissed his teeth looking down at Markieff's hand. "I wasn't talking to you. I was talking to my wife."

Markieff bit down on his bottom lip, trying to suppress the urge to knock Aaron out. He could smell the liquor on Aaron's breath and knew it was the liquor giving him that courage. Stepping back, Markieff eyed Aaron up and down. He knew he could easily punish him. But with Kian in the house, he gave Aaron a free pass.

"Lucky, I will catch up with you later." Markieff said to Serenity.

"Nigga, you won't be doing no catching up with my wife. So if I was you, I would get the fuck on." Aaron instructed.

Markieff rubbed the back of his head. "Yo, when you go in the house make sure you go kiss your son good night. While you're at it, tell him thank you for saving your fucking life," he said through gritted teeth. "Like I said, Lucky Charm, we will catch up later. Don't forget to tell Mr. Benny I asked about him."

"I already did. He wanted to talk to you. Let me grab my phone so I can call him for you." Serenity informed him.

"Nah, let me bounce before my fist accidently punches your husband in the face." Markieff stated in a serious tone. "Kian got my number, pass it on to Mr. Benny for me."

It took Aaron a few seconds to comprehend what was just said. He moved towards Markieff with his fist balled up and said, "What you just say?"

Serenity quickly jumped in front of him before anything could pop off. Knowing Markieff from their younger days, Serenity was aware of the damage he would do to Aaron if they fought. As long as she'd been with Aaron she never witnessed him in a confrontation, and wasn't sure if he could even hold his own. To save the embarrassment she had to step in.

"Bae, just go inside." Serenity pleaded, looking Aaron in his eyes.

"Yea, take your ass in the house," Markieff taunted."

"Kieff, chill," Serenity yelled, giving Markieff a stern look.

Throwing his hands up, Markieff stepped back. "For you, I will. I'm gone Ma, just hit me up later."

"Ok," Serenity said. Aaron finally went inside, but she stood there and watched Markieff get into his car and pull out her driveway. She then walked into the house and closed the door. She closed her eyes and rested her back against the door. But moments later, she felt Aaron's hands around her neck. Her eyes quickly popped open and she smacked the shit out of him backing him up.

"Boy, have you lost your damn mind?" Serenity screamed.

Aaron staggered back a little but regained his balance with the help of the wall. "Why was that nigga in my house?"

"First of all, he wasn't in the house. Second, he was doing something your ass should've been doing today. He was nice enough to come get Kian and took him to football practice." Serenity rubbed her neck, still stunned that Aaron actually put his hands on her.

"You fuck that nigga?" Aaron slurred.

"Nigga, are you listening to me. I said he wasn't in the house. But since you in here asking questions, I thought you had to go to New York for work?"

"Shit," Aaron cursed himself. He started walking, "I did, but my flight was delayed and I wasn't trying to sit around the airport. I told James to reschedule that shit." He quickly lied. It wasn't until then he asked himself why he came home when he had other places to crash for the night. He should have known Serenity was going to question him. He cursed himself, knowing he fucked up but he was pissed at Nene and wasn't thinking straight.

Serenity knew Aaron was full of shit and was lying. She let out a snicker and left the conversation at that. She followed behind Aaron stomping up the stairs.

"Yo, chill with all that noise my head hurt."

Doing the opposite, Serenity got louder. She walked into her room and picked up her phone then went back downstairs so she could call Treasure. Aaron was steading yelling at Serenity, but she ignored him.

"Is that Aaron I hear in the background? I thought you said he was going out of town? Did you stand me up?" Treasure asked once she was on the phone.

"Fuck that nigga," Serenity snarled. She was disgusted at the man he has become. She doesn't know when her marriage took a turn for the worst, but she hated the direction it was going in.

"Well damn, where did that come from?" Treasure inquired. Out of the year she's known Serenity, she never heard her speak in that type of tone referring to Aaron.

Serenity went outside and stood on her back patio. She let out a deep breath and said, "I think Aaron's cheating on me."

"Girl, shut the hell up," Treasure laughed.

"Te, I'm being serious."

When Treasure heard the sadness in Serenity's voice she stopped laughing. "What makes you think that?"

"He hasn't been fucking me for one. Then, he's been going out of town a lot more for work. I don't know, but my gut is telling me something is going on. I don't have proof but I can't shake this damn feeling."

"Wow, I didn't think Aaron would do you like that."

"Yea, me either." Serenity sadly said, looking up at her wedding photo hanging on the wall.

Chapter 3

"Dad, why I can't stay the night with you?" Mykel whined.

"Because, it's a school night."

"So. You can take me to school. I don't want to go home, I want to stay with you." Mykel slammed his back against the seat and crossed his arms over his chest.

Markieff glanced over to Mykel and hated to see the sad look painted on his face. Pulling up to the house Markieff spotted Shana, Mykel's mother sitting on the steps with two of her friends. Soon as the car was in park Mykel jump out, slamming the door shut and stomped his way into the house. Markieff got out shaking his head. He grabbed Mykel's bag from the backseat and walked it to Shana.

"What the fuck you do to my son?" Shana snarled, snatching the bag from Markieff's hands.

"I didn't do shit to him. He mad he had to come back here." Markieff informed her.

"Yea whatever." Shana said, turning around.

Markieff had enough of Shana's attitude. So doing something he should have been done, he was putting his foot down.

"You know what, fuck this. Mykel, come on you staying with me." Markieff bumped Shana going into her house. "Kel, come on. Make sure you grab your backpack for school," he yelled again.

Mykel happily rushed down the stairs. "For real, I can go with you?"

"Yea, let's..." Markieff started to say.

"No, you can't go." Shana cut Markieff off. "Why would you tell him that."

"Because he's going with me. Clearly, he doesn't want to fucking stay here. He hasn't seen me in months, the least you can do is let him chill with me. Bad enough I had to beg for you to let him play football just so I could spend extra time with him. You got this new nigga and lost your damn mind, forgetting who the fuck I am." Markieff clenched his jaws, giving her a stern look.

"My man doesn't have shit to do with this. You're the one that changed up," Shana reminded him.

"I know your ass not mad about that when you have a...You know what, we not doing this," Markieff said, getting off the subject. "Look, I'm done playing your games. I'm spending time with my son. So, fuck all that shit you talking right now." With that, Markieff told Mykel to get in the car.

Shana stood there and blankly stared as Markieff walked away. She still loved him and knew she was selfish for trying to keep Mykel away from him thinking she was punishing Markieff. She was bitter and Mykel was a pawn to control his life.

"Yo, I'm sorry you had to hear that. I shouldn't have come at your mother like that while you was standing there." Markieff apologized. He prides himself on not fighting in front of Mykel. He didn't want him seeing that type of stuff thinking it was ok.

"It's cool dad. I know she can piss you off sometimes."

Markieff couldn't help the snicker that slipped out his mouth. "Watch your mouth boy. But yea, she does but I still shouldn't have done that in front of you."

"Can Kian come over since you cool with his mom?"

"Next time son. Tonight, I just want it to be me and you, ard?"

"Ard," Mykel agreed.

At the mention of Kian's name Markieff remember he needed to call Mr. Benny. He took his phone out and scrolled his contacts and found Kian's number.

"What's up coach?" Kian answered.

"Ky is your mother around?" Markieff asked, but then he could hear yelling. "Is that her yelling?"

Kian let out a sigh. "Yea, her and my dad been arguing since he got home."

"Take her the phone" Markieff said in a stern tone.

The line got silent and Markieff could hear Kian getting closer to Serenity and Aaron. His blood started to boil hearing what Aaron was saying. It further pissed him off that Aaron would say what he said, knowing his son was in the house.

"Mom, the phone," Kian's shaky voice said, extending his phone toward Serenity.

Serenity went to reach for the phone, but Aaron snatched it from Kian.

"Who is this?" Aaron snarled.

Markieff normally would have checked Aaron, but he really needed to talk to Serenity and didn't want any conflict between him and Aaron right now. He covered the phone and whispered to Mykel. "Say you need to ask Serenity something," he instructed before passing the phone.

"Who the fuck is this," Aaron yelled again.

Hearing Aaron's tone, Mykel fumbled over his words getting a little nervous. "Hey...hey Mr. Aaron. I wanted to ask Mrs. Serenity if Kian could come over tomorrow."

Not saying a word Aaron passed Serenity the phone. After that, he headed for the door and left. Serenity closed her eyes letting out a frustrated breath of air.

"Hello," she answered.

"Here daddy, it's her," Mykel said, giving back the phone.

"You good? Do I need to come over there?" Markieff asked out of concern.

"No, you don't have to do all that. I can handle Aaron. But, what's up?"

"Yea ard, if you say so. I was calling to get Benny's number."

"Oh, that's it?" Serenity joked.

"Yea. What else I'm calling your big ass head for?"

"Nothing fool, I'm just joking. The number is 215-838-4383."

"Bet. I'm just pulling up to my complex. I will holla at you later."

"Ok."

Markieff dialed Benny's number as he walked into his apartment. The phone rang twice and Benny's deep voice came across the line.

"Hello." Benny boomed on the other ended.

"Papa B. What's good old head?" Markieff laughed.

"My youngin'. Markieff, glad to hear your voice. How have you been?" Benny questioned.

"Hanging in there. Other than some baby mama drama, no complaints." Markieff joked.

"I hear you. Damn, what it's been almost twelve years?"

"Yea, just about."

"How's your parents?"

"My mother is good. Pops, he...he died a few years back."

"Sorry to hear that. My condolences."

"Thanks. You know me and the old man never really connected. Especially after we moved to Florida." Markieff paused for a second. "You know I heard what he said the day we moved. After that, I was too scared to even reach out once I got older, thinking you hated me or something. I think bumping into Serenity was a sign that I needed to talk to you."

"Mar, you know I loved you like my own. It wasn't no secret me and your father didn't see eye to eye. I understood why he hated me. Just know that had nothing to do with you. I wish you didn't feel that way son."

"Thank you for always being there for me Papa B. Now that we got that out the way, what you doing tomorrow old man? Want to get lunch or something?"

"I'm out of town on business and will be gone all week. I'm having a cookout Saturday for Labor Day. You know, the last cookout for the summer and back to school bash for the youngins. You should come and we can catch up then." Benny suggested.

"Sounds good to me. See you then."

Markieff ended his call with Benny and went to Mykel's room to check on him. "What you playing?" He asked, flopping down on the bed.

"Just Case. You want to play Madden?" Mykel asked.

"Let's go." Markieff said, grabbing the extra controller to the Playstation 4.

After a few rounds of playing the game, Markieff finally called it quits. He retired to his room after taking a shower. As he was laying across his bed his thoughts drifted to Serenity. He was mad he never told her how he felt about her when they were younger. But, with Benny looking at him like a son he felt it wasn't the right thing to do. Just as he was about to call Serenity, his phone vibrated in his hand. He let out a frustrated breath.

"What," he scoffed answering the phone.

"Can you come open the door?" Shana asked.

"What the hell you doing here? Nah, you can stay your dumbass out there." Markieff got off his bed and walked over to his window and looked out of it. True indeed, Shana's car was parked at his door.

"Please," Shana begged.

Markieff ended the call and started to head downstairs. He opened his door just as Shana was getting out her car. He stepped out his door and Shana turned around and smiled seeing him standing there. She closed her car door and walked up to him tugging on the bottom of his shirt.

"I'm sorry ok. I love you and I just hate that you cut me off." Shana sobbed.

Markieff smacked her hand away. "I don't need to hear this shit. You wanted that other nigga and soon as I moved the fuck on, you wanted that old thing back. It doesn't work like that Ma. We not about to do that back and forth shit. We too old for that shit. You played me thinking Khalil was going to make it big in the NBA and that nigga didn't even get drafted. Then you had that other nigga you thought was a fucking kingpin, but that nigga turned out to be a fuck boy. I had to save your ass from him God knows how many times. Then, you got this new nigga and took my son away from me. I'm getting sick of my son being around all these dudes. Keep it up, I'm going to take you to court for full custody." Markieff said, through gritted teeth.

"Just take me back and we can end all this," Shana said, rubbing her hand across his dick. She smirked at him when she felt it growing from her touch. "Just take me back and we can be a family. I miss you."

Markieff bit down on his bottom lip trying to fight the temptation. It wasn't easy when you're a man with months worth of backup. He closed his eyes trying to make his dick go down, but the way Shana was massaging it though his pants he couldn't help it. He grabbed hold of her hand and dragged her into the house, knowing he was going to regret what was about to happen.

"I miss you," Shana said.

"Kill that, I don't want to hear it." Markieff took her into his room and turned on the radio. He took off his clothes and soon as his hard dick sprang from his boxers, Shana dropped to her knees. "Fuuuckkk," he moaned as she deep throated him.

Shana bobbed her head up and down taking every inch of him to the back of her throat. Markieff tilted his head back closing his eyes. Shana sucked on the tip of his dick and her hands moved up and down jacking him off.

"You like that bae?" Shana asked between sucking and licking his length.

Markieff didn't answer her. He placed his hand on her head guiding it up and down. After a few more minutes of getting head Markieff was ready to fuck.

"Aye, bend over." Markieff informed her.

Shana got up and pulled down her pants. As she was getting undressed Markieff took the time to go over to his dresser and grabbed a condom.

"You don't want to feel me raw?" Shana purred.

"Nah I'm good love, turn around." He said, bending her over. He entered her from the back. He gave her a deep long strokes.

"Yess, Mar. Just like that baby. Get this pussy," Shana yelled at the feel of Markieff pounding her insides.

Markieff wanted to get this quick nut so he fucked her hard and fast. He showed her no mercy as he punished her pussy. He placed his hand in the small of her back pushing her down further going deeper.

"Fuck," Markeiff grunted feeling his load ready to explode. He gripped her hips and picked up his pace going faster and deeper. He closed his eyes and

Serenity's face popped in his head. Just like that, he busted his nut and opened his eyes.

"Damn, where the fuck that come from?" He asked himself, wondering why Serenity's face popped in his head in the middle of fucking his baby mama.

***

Later that night, Markieff found himself sitting on his couch blankly staring at the television. He didn't know why he kept letting Shana back in when she didn't deserve his time. He could hear footsteps coming down the stairs and knew they belonged to Shana. He reached up and grabbed his beer taking a sip.

"What are you doing down here?" Shana questioned.

"I needed to come clear my head." Markieff dryly answered.

"What's wrong?" Shana asked, sitting down on his lap.

Markieff quickly lifted her up and sat her next to him and moved over a little. "I think you need to leave before Mykel wakes up."

"What!"

"Look, you got what you wanted from me and I appreciate you for helping me work that nut out, but you can go now." Markieff harshly stated.

"Wow. Last time you acted like this towards me it was another bitch in the picture. So what, you done got you a flavor of the month and I'm back on the shelf until you get tired of her?"

"See, there you go running your mouth. It's nobody in the picture. I'm just not doing this shit with you no more. Tonight was the last time so I hope you enjoyed it." Markieff grabbed his beer and headed towards the stairs. "Lock my door when you leave."

Shana sat there staring at Markieff wondering if this was really the last time. He said that time and time before, but for some reason it felt real this go around.

The next morning, Markieff woke up and got Mykel ready for school before he headed to work. It was his first day on the job and he wasn't trying to be late.

"Kel, let's go boy," Markieff yelled.

"Coming daddy." Moments later, Mykel came running down the stairs. "Ready," he smiled.

"About time." "Here," Markieff handed Mykel his breakfast biscuit and juice.

They headed out the house all smiles, but Markieff stopped abruptly. "What the fuck," he yelled seeing his car severely damaged.

"Dang daddy, who did this to your car?"

"I don't know. But go in the house. I need to call Ms. Serenity to see if she can take you to school." Markieff then pulled out his phone and quickly dialed Kian's number since he failed to get Serenity's.

"Good morning Uncle Markieff." Kian beamed when he answered the phone.

"Hey Ki. Are you near your mother?"

"Yea, we about to leave out the house. You need to talk to her."

"Yes please." Markieff could hear Kian calling Serenity to the phone and waited for her to come on the line.

"Boy, why you didn't call my phone?" Serenity asked coming on the line.

"I don't have your number. But look, can you please come pick up Mykel for me and take him to school?"

"Yea, where are you?"

"I stay over on Winchester Ave not too far from you. My house number is 3343."

"Ard, I'm on the way."

"Lucky, I appreciate it." Markieff thanked her.

"Boy hush. See you soon."

Markieff shook his head taking another look at his car. All the windows was shattered, all the tires was slashed, and his headlights was broken. In bold letters was the words, Fuck You. From that alone, he knew this was Shana's handy work.

Five minutes later, Serenity was pulling up. Markieff yelled for Mykel to come outside.

"Wow, is this your car?" Serenity asked, walking around it.

"Yea," he dryly answered.

"You pissed somebody off."

"Nah, just a bitter ass female being fucking petty. Now I need to call my homeboy to come pick this up and take it to the shop. Damn, I'm going to be late for fucking work and this my first damn day. Thank God I been with the company for a minute and just transferring over."

"Yea. Well, let me go before I be late getting them off to school."

Mykel finally came out the house and Serenity raced him to the car. Markieff smiled as he watched. Taking out his phone hating to have to call his friend. He knew he was going to clown him for this and wasn't going to let him hear the end of it.

Markieff went into the house to wait for his ride. Sitting on the couch, he called Shana's number but she didn't answer.

"You petty as shit. Why would you do that shit to my car knowing our son had to see it. You wonder why I won't take your crazy ass back. You lucky I don't put my hands on females, because that shit is grounds to beat your ass." Markieff snapped.

"Bruh, I know that's not your fucking whip beat up like that?" Lamont laughed.

"Yea man," Markieff shook his head.

"Damn, let me guess. Shana ass done that shit. I told you when we was in college to leave that crazy chick alone."

"Yea you did, but it was too late. I was already in love and Mykel was on the way."

"Nah, that ass was pussy whipped." Lamont continued to laugh.

Markieff laughed. "Fuck you."

"Come on before we late for work." Lamont tapped his chest.

Chapter 4

S erenity made it to work with ten minutes to spare. Using the backdoor for work, Serenity stopped in the employee lounge to put her food into the refrigerator. When she entered, Treasure was inside making coffee.

"Hey girl," Serenity dryly spoke.

"Hey boo. Why the long face?" Treasure asked out of concern.

"Girl, I don't know what's going on but me and Aaron been arguing a lot lately. He changed and I'm not feeling this bullshit with him. I am getting sick of this shit. I am not built for this. I am trying to stick to my vows, but I am not trying to be with nobody who don't want to be with me. Bad enough Kian is paying attention and sees what is going on."

Treasure walked over and hugged Serenity. "Aww boo, I am sorry you are feeling like this. Maybe you two need to sit down and have a talk." Treasure suggested.

"Yea, I will try if his ass can stay home. If he's not going out of town for work, he is coming home late. I just don't know anymore." Serenity sighed.

Moments later, two of the other tellers walked into the lounge gossiping like always.

"Girl, I wonder if he's single. He is fine as hell with his yellow ass. And lawd, those uniform pants fit his ass good. I saw that print and baby he is blessed." One of the tellers said.

Treasure raised her brows and jumped in their conversation. "Who you two talking about?

"The new guard. Listen heffa, stay away I saw him first." The teller named Toni said in a serious tone.

"Umm, a little too pressed aren't we," Treasure teased.

"Very," Serenity added. "See you up front," Serenity told Treasure. Just as she opened the door, somebody was coming in.

"And this is the lounge," Lamont said walking in with Markieff.

Serenity's mouth hung opened, shocked to see who the officer was. "Markieff," she called out.

"Oh damn, don't tell me you work here too Lucky." Markieff smiled.

"You two know each other?" Lamont asked.

"Oh yea, me and Lucky go way back. Damn man, your ass could have given me a ride to work too." Markieff smiled.

Serenity playfully hit his arm. "I didn't even know you worked here."

"Umm, the uniform. I had it on when you picked up Kel."

"Boy, I wasn't even paying attention to you." Serenity shook her head disappointed she didn't even notice Markieff in his uniform.

Treasure couldn't help but notice the disappointed look plastered on Toni's face and had to say something. "Humph, seems like somebody is off limits," Treasure laughed, looking over to Toni. "Serenity are you going to introduce me to your friend?"

"No," Serenity laughed, knowing Treasure was being petty.

"Ugh, so damn rude. I'm Treasure," she introduced herself, extending her hand to Markieff.

"Nice to meet you." Markieff laughed.

Toni stepped forward and stood in front of Markieff. "I'm..." She started to say, but Treasure interrupted her introduction.

"A non-fucking factor that nobody asked about," Treasure rudely cut her off.

Markieff and Lamont couldn't help but snicker.

"Yo, you so damn stupid for that," Lamont pointed out. He tapped Markieff and told him to follow him.

Markieff glanced at Serenity before walking out. He could tell something was wrong with her. He went over to her and grabbed her hand. "You good?"

Serenity quickly nodded her head up and down. "Yea, yea. I'm good."

"Mar, we gotta go make rounds bruh." Lamont called out.

"I will come check on you when I'm done. You know I know you and you're lying. Something's up and we going to talk about it like the old days."

Serenity couldn't fight the smile that grew on her face. "Ok." When Serenity turned around to say something to Treasure she saw the smug look on Toni face. "You have something you got to say?"

"Nope, not at all. Come on Cindy, so we can start our work day," Toni said, waving to the other teller.

"Girl please. You're going up front to sit on your damn phone lurking on Facebook," Treasure scoffed, putting Toni on blast.

Toni stuck up her middle finger as she made her way out the door.

Once Serenity fixed her cup of tea she went to her station up front. Passing a few of the ladies that worked in the bank Serenity overheard their conversation about the new guard. All she could do was shake her head knowing Markieff was going to be the new piece of eye candy around the bank. Making it to her computer Serenity powered it on and logged on to her account. Out of the corner of her eyes she could see Treasure staring. She tried to ignore her but couldn't, so she turned to face her with a smirk on her face. Serenity knew why Treasure was staring, but still had to mess with her.

"Ugh, do you have something to say?" Serenity joked.

"Sure do. What's the deal with you and Markieff? That man was looking at you like he was about to bend that ass over and give you the business."

Serenity's eyes got big and she quickly looked around to make sure nobody heard Treasure's comment. "You are a mess," she laughed. She grabbed her cup and took a sip of tea.

"Umm, stop stalling and talk." Treasure rushed her.

"Ugh ok. I mean it's nothing major. We grew up together. He and my dad were actually close. He helped my dad with a lot of things around the house and shop. Then he started going out collecting money for my dad when he did sports pools and shit at one of the bars he owns. They gambled a lot and Markeiff was his mini me."

"Sooo, that nigga was like a brother to you?"

"I wouldn't say all that."

"Oh, y'all fucked huh?"

Serenity reached over and hit Treasure's arm. "I can't with you. No, we never fucked. I don't think he looked at me that way back then. I think he had a crush on my sister Egypt. And speaking of her, let me call her ass," Serenity said, changing up the subject. She then reached over and grabbed her phone and dialed her sister's number.

"Yes Serenity," Egypt answered the phone.

"You said Aaron didn't have no meetings out of town this week. You know I am trying to get my marriage back on track."

"Look, I'm his assistant not his damn keeper. He didn't have anything, but I think this recent job was a last-minute thing."

"Umm humm," Serenity hummed. "Did you go too?"

"Girl no. I'm home with my man."

"Have you noticed any of them females being extra around Aaron at the office?"

"No, why you ask that?"

Taking a deep breath Serenity said, "I think he's cheating." The line got silent and Serenity pulled it from her ear to look at it. "Egypt, you're still there?"

"Yea, I'm here girl. I had to make sure I heard you right. This is Aaron we are talking about. Ok, as much as I hate his black ass, he not stupid and wouldn't fuck up a good thing he got at home. Plus, that damn man worships the ground you walk on. Why do you think he's cheating?"

"For one, he hasn't touched me in God knows when. Then, every time I turn around his ass going away for work. I hate he got that fucking promotion because this shit is coming between our marriage. And for your information he used to worship the ground I walk on. This nigga has done a whole three-sixty and barely acknowledges my ass. Thinking about it this change may even have been before the promotion. It's just that now this shit is more obvious to me."

"Oh my God Te, you can't be serious. Don't be one of those wives that panic and starts assuming shit because her man is out here grinding making sure his family is good. Tell me this, other than him not fucking you and staying away from home, do you have any evidence to prove he's cheating?"

"No, but his change of behavior says it all. I feel that shit in my gut." Serenity exclaimed.

"Girl, that man is not doing anything. You're just over thinking. Reading all those books and watching Lifetime got your head messed up. Maybe when he gets back, you two need to go out or something. I can keep Kian for you."

"I guess." Serenity sighed. A customer came in and was headed towards Serenity's window. "Look, I will call you when I get off. I have a customer coming."

"Ok sis. And don't stress yourself over nothing." Egypt told her.

"Easier said then done," Serenity said to herself. She ended her call and tended to the customer that came in. When she was done, she finished up a few things that needed to be done on a few accounts she had. For the remainder of the day, she was able to keep her mind off Aaron and what he might be doing.

"We ordering something for lunch?" Treasure asked Serenity.

"Nah, I brought something from home. Matter fact, I'm going to warm my food up. You need something from the back?"

"Yea, can you bring me back a Milky Way and a Pepsi?" Treasure requested. "I will just get something off the food truck in a few."

As Serenity made her way to the break room, she locked eyes with Markieff. He was sitting at his desk talking to a few of the other ladies that worked in the bank. His eyes followed Serenity as she walked by him. She then heard him excusing himself and follow her to the break room. When he walked in they locked eyes again. The room then filled with awkward silence. Serenity grabbed her food and placed it in the microwave before going over to the vending machine to get Treasure's snacks. Markieff then came over and stood behind her.

"What you getting me?" He asked getting closer to her.

Serenity chuckled. "Umm, nothing."

The break room doors opened and Toni walked in. She turned her nose up seeing how close Markieff was standing behind Serenity. They both looked at Toni but ignored her. Markieff went back to bugging Serenity.

"Stop playing and get me a pack of M&M's," Markieff requested, talking to Serenity.

"Boy, I am not buying you shit," Serenity snickered.

"I will get it for you," Toni quickly offered.

Markieff smiled and said, "Nah, it's cool. I'm good love."

Serenity snickered and walked back over to the microwave to grab her food.

"So Serenity, how is your husband." Toni asked, trying to throw salt thinking Serenity was hitting on Markieff.

"You're such a bitch. You trying to throw shade but news flash, Markieff knows I am married. So, fall back." Serenity scoffed. When she walked passed Toni she made sure to bump into her hard.

"Aye, watch that shit," Toni warned her.

"Or what?" Serenity dared her to make a move.

Toni sucked her teeth. "Girl, stop it. You trying to show off in front of him knowing you're not about that life."

Serenity placed her things on the table. She was getting sick of everyone trying her not knowing she wasn't one to play with. Just as Serenity was about to make her move, Markieff peeped what she was doing and grabbed her.

"Lucky, not here. Don't risk your job over this broad." Markieff said, wrapping Serenity up in his arms.

"Let her ass go and watch she get that ass beat." Toni said.

As much as he wanted to let her loose he didn't want to risk his job either. How would it look that security was in the break room watching a fight and didn't try to stop it? Because he sure was going to let Serenity work Toni's big mouth.

"Get off me, I'm good." Serenity pushed away. "And as for you, don't let this cute face and my kindness fool you. I will fuck you up then check you in for medical attention. So you need to thank Markieff for saving your life." Serenity snapped. She grabbed her food and Treasure's things and walked back up front.

Treasure noticed the frown on Serenity's face and pondered what happened between her leaving from up front to the break room. "Girl, what the hell wrong with you?"

"That bitch Toni. Her thirsty ass mad Markieff not paying her ugly ass any attention and tried me. She told me I was putting up a front in front of him. So of course, that North Philly came out of me. Markieff ass grabbed me before I could reach out and touch that hoe."

"Girl, do you want me to do it?" Treasure raised her brows.

"No. Markieff is right, that bitch not worth losing my coins over."

"Shit, you would be good. Aaron would take care of you if you got fired."

Serenity sucked her teeth. "Fuck that nigga too."

Treasure couldn't help but side eye Serenity. At first, she thought she was just being over dramatic about Aaron, but now she can tell she wasn't. "You really think he's cheating?"

"I don't know what to think. It's...He just giving me that vibe and I can't shake it. But look, I need some fresh air. You want me to get your food from the truck?"

"Yea. Bring me a Chicken Gyro." Treasure dug in her bag and got her wallet getting the money for Serenity.

Serenity took the money and headed outside. Stepping out she looked down the block and saw the long line at the food truck. "Fuck," she cursed. Looking in the opposite direction she saw Markieff pacing back and forth yelling into his phone.

"Look, I told you that shit is dead between us. I just want to take care of my son without the fucking headache. And I know it was you that fucked up my car." Markieff paused for a second then started yelling again. "What the fuck you mean I can't see my son...Hello..hello," Markieff repeated into the phone.

He then pulled the phone from his ear and eyed it, seeing Shana hung up. "Fuck," he screamed angrily.

"You ok?" Serenity asked, walking up to him.

"Nah. My bitter ass baby mama just told me I couldn't see my fucking son. She mad because I don't want to play her fucking side nigga and shit. She keeps forgetting she broke up with me back then thinking she was going to get her an NBA player and shit. Even after that, she was fucking with these fucking lames not even thinking about my ass. But all of a sudden, she wants a nigga."

"Come walk with me to the food truck. I may buy you something this time," Serenity joked, playfully bumping him with her hips.

"You better," Markieff laughed. "Ugh," he sighed loudly. "Why females so damn petty when they don't get their way, man?"

"Not all females the same. Shit, why do niggas cheat when they have a wife at home," Serenity blurted out, not meaning to.

Markieff stopped walking and grabbed Serenity's arm stopping her. "That nigga cheating on you?"

"No, I was just saying in general." Serenity quickly lied.

"Yea, ard. Your ass lying but I'm not going to get all in your business."

"Whatever boy." Serenity brushed it off. They made it to the food truck and got in line. "You know, if you need help seeing Mykel I can help you with that."

"How?" Markieff raised his brows.

"Well, it's going to be on some sneaky shit and Mykel can't tell. I can just ask Shana to let him come over on the weekend. She's not going to think anything of it, because she doesn't know we know each other. Mykel has to keep it between us and not tell her he saw you or anything."

"He won't. I don't even think he likes staying there, man. Something is up with her punk ass boyfriend, I can feel it."

"Yea, I know bull. They call him Rusty. I think he from West Philly."

Markieff kissed his teeth. "Fuck that nigga."

"I hear you. I will set something up this weekend." Serenity was next in line and ordered Treasure's food.

"Lucky, thanks for looking out." Markieff said. "I don't know why she loves pressing my fucking buttons. She got like this before when I was talking to this chick and called herself moving out here with that nigga. I would have been back, but I had to wait for my transfer and a spot to stay."

"Yea, I remember when they moved here. She used to live next door to me. That's how Kian and Mykel became friends. It didn't help that they were in the same class at school."

"Yea, that shit killed me when they moved. At first, her ass didn't even tell me where they moved to. So for a year I didn't know. But Lamont saw her ass out at Franklin Mills and called me." Markieff said, shaking his head.

"Damn, I didn't know she did all that. That's fucked up man."

"Yea, now she is trying this bullshit again."

"Don't worry, I got you." Serenity nudged him.

"I know Lucky," Markieff winked.

The food was ready and Serenity grabbed it. They walked back to the bank making small talk. When they got to front of the bank, Markieff stopped and sat down on the bench that was out front.

"See you inside. I'm going to sit out here for a while." Markieff told her.

"You good? I mean if you want to talk, I'm here for you. Like you said, even though we been apart for a long time, I'm still your Lucky Charm," she smiled.

"I know. I just need some alone time."

Serenity nodded her head and gave him his privacy. When she got back inside Treasure was on the phone yelling at it.

"Girl, who got you going off?" Serenity asked, placing her food on her desk.

"Ugh, one of Junior's dummies in my inbox asking why the fuck he texting me. Like bitch, go ask your nigga. I mean, if her ass could read she clearly sees I'm not entertaining his ass. These females need to learn how to check their nigga, not the female."

The entrance doors opened pulling her attention away from Treasure. It was Markieff walking back inside with sadness written all over his face.

"What's wrong with your boo?" Treasure asked.

Serenity reached over and hit Treasure's arm. "Cut that out. He got baby mama drama. Oh, and guess who his baby mama is?"

"You?" Treasure continued to joke.

"No fool. Shana."

"Shana as in Mykel mother?"

"Yep. And, she is petty as hell. She called him telling him he can't see Mykel since he cut her off with the dick. She wants him to play side nigga and shit."

"You know if Rusty finds out he getting played, that nigga going to cut the fuck up. She better know who her nigga is. But wait, didn't she tell us her baby daddy was dead or something? Remember when we first met her she was saying they moved from Delaware and her son's father was killed?"

"She probably did, but I wasn't paying her any attention."

Moments later, they spotted Toni and one of her sidekicks coming from the side door. They went over to the office the security officers use. Serenity rolled her eyes and chuckled.

"They trying too damn hard. Lamont even said they was being extra. So you know it's true when that nigga points that shit out." Treasure stated.

"Right," Serenity said in agreement.

Thanks to the paperwork Serenity had to finish she kept herself busy. It helped keeping her mind off her problems for the moment. Once the work day was over Serenity grabbed her things and hurried out the door. Going out the door she was going to stop by the security office to see if Markieff needed a ride.

"Knock, knock," she said, tapping on the door. When she had Markieff's attention she asked if he needed a ride back home.

Markieff shook his head, saying no. "Nah, I'm good."

"Ok, well see you later." With that, Serenity hightailed it out of there.

Chapter 5

I t's been a few days and Serenity was surprised Aaron was still home. It was Saturday and they were actually headed to Kian's football game as a family. After that they was going to her parent's house for a cookout.

"Dad, I'm so happy you're here to see me play. I'm going to score three touchdowns for you," Kian happily said.

"I'm glad I'm here too baby boy. I wouldn't miss this for the world." Aaron replied.

Serenity couldn't help but chuckle. Aaron took his eyes from the road and peered over to Serenity. "Something funny?"

"Yea, you." Serenity snickered.

"And what's that supposed to mean? I mean damn, I'm here right? Seems like I can't do shit without you complaining and I am getting sick of it."

"Really Aaron. You doing this in front of Kian?" Serenity pointed out.

Aaron looked up in the rearview mirror and saw Kian had on his headphones. "He can't hear us."

They pulled up to the football field and Kian didn't waste any time jumping out. He heard Aaron and he hated that his dad talked to his mom that way. He learned from his grandfather a long time ago he was his mother's protector, but he just didn't know how to protect her from his father.

"Coach, where is Mykel?" Serenity heard Kian ask Markieff, causing her to look his way.

Aaron's phone then went off, pulling Serenity's attention to him.

"Don't look at me like that. Let me just see what they want." Aaron quickly said.

Serenity sucked her teeth and grabbed her bag from the backseat. She then rolled her eyes walking away from the car. Aaron waited until she was a good distance away to call the person back that called.

"Oh, now you can pick up a phone." Nene hissed on the other end of the phone.

"Why do you keep calling me? I told you it was fucking over," Aaron loudly whispered into his phone.

"I said I was sorry. I miss you baby" Nene cried on the other end of the phone.

"Yea, well you should have thought about that shit before you got slick at the mouth.

"Come on now, you know that's how I am. I am just sick of you playing with my emotions. You swear you don't love her and promised me you were leaving. You keep saying you staying because of your son, but I still don't understand. You leaving won't stop you from being his damn father. I'm getting fed up with this shit. Why should she have it all when I'm the one you love?"

"Look, I will come by later and we can talk. Right now, I'm at my son's football game and after that I have to go to this damn cookout. Once I'm done I will get my brother to cover for me or something."

"You promise?"

Aaron could hear Nene talking, but his eyes were glued on Serenity.

"A, do you hear me?" Nene shouted.

"Yea, yea, I promise. I have to go." Aaron quickly ended the call as he watched Serenity and Markieff.

He wasn't feeling how close she was walking with him. When he saw him interacting with Kian, that touched a nerve. Markieff and Kian took off running racing to the field. Aaron then jogged up to Serenity and grabbed her arm, spinning her around to face him.

"What's wrong with you?" Serenity asked, trying to snatch away from Aaron's tight grip.

"You fucking him?" He asked through gritted teeth.

"Are you smoking something? Because clearly, you lost your fucking mind," Serenity hissed. "What, your guilt eating you up and now you trying to accuse me of something?"

Aaron sucked his teeth releasing his grip from her arm. "What are you talking about?" He asked, playing dumb.

"You know exactly what I'm talking about. You changed ever since you got that punk ass promotion. I know you fucking somebody else."

"Yea well if you know, why you still here?" Aaron boldly blurted out.

Serenity mouth hung opened, baffled that Aaron was bold enough to say what he did. She felt the tears burning her eyes but fought like hell keeping them at bay. She wasn't about to show him he hurt her. But she will admit, his words stung like hell. She pushed him out her way as she made her way over to the bleachers and sat down. Her leg bounced up and down hating that she was right. Although Aaron didn't come out and say it, he lowkey admitted to cheating. Words speak volumes and she heard and felt his.

Markieff looked up to the stands and saw the scowl plastered on Serenity's face. He then looked over to Aaron who was busy on his phone.

"Mont, I'm going over here for a second." Makieff yelled out to Lamont. He walked down the field with his phone in his hand sending a text to Serenity.

Markieff: Yo, what the fuck wrong with your face? You was just good a minute ago.

After hitting the send button he peered over to the stands, waiting for Serenity to read her message and text back. It didn't take long because his phone was going off within seconds.

Lucky Charm: Nothing.

Markieff chuckled and left it as that. He went back over to the team. Soon as he got over there, Kian had run down the field ready to catch the ball that was in the air.

"Go Ki, go." Markieff cheered loudly, running the length of the field. Once he scored the touchdown, Markieff jumped up and down. "That's my boy. Yes, Ki." He then looked up to stands and saw Aaron was mugging him. Serenity was smiling again and that's all that mattered.

"Coach, did you see me. I was gone like Antonio Brown." Kian said, referring to Pittsburgh Steelers wide receiver.

"You sure was. Good job." Markieff held his hand up waiting for a high five.

"That touchdown was for you," Kian said. "I just wish Mykel was here. His mama tripping."

"Yea, she is." Markieff agreed. "Hey, don't worry about that little man. I need you to go on defense for me. Go tell Nate to come out and get that ball back for me."

"Got you coach." Kian ran back on the field.

The other team got two plays in but the next play, Kian did what Markieff asked him to do. He caught an interception and ran back for a touchdown. Markieff could hear Serenity cheering in the stands and again Aaron was quiet as a mouse looking on. Kian ran off the field and right up to Markieff.

"I did it coach." He said, giving Markieff a high five.

"Good job Ki. Go get some water and take a breather. You're going back out in a little." Markieff felt his phone going off in his pocket and saw Serenity was texting him.

Lucky Charm: Look, I need to go. Can you catch a ride with Lamont and let me use your rental car to go? Kian can go home with Aaron.

Markieff: Yea, I got you.

Markieff stuffed his phone back into his pocket. "Ki, go get that water."

Kian walked over to the water table and looked upon the crowd of people. He was searching for Aaron and Serenity, but they weren't in their seats. He scanned the crowd again and found them standing near the restrooms yelling at each other. He let out sigh, shaking his head. After drinking a cup of water he joined his team on the sidelines.

Lamont noticed the discomfort on Kian's face. He walked over placing his hand on his shoulders. "What's up little man?"

"Nothing. Where is coach Markieff?"

"Oh, he went to the restroom." Lamont answered.

"I'm ready to go back in."

"Ard, next play get back in there."

Lamont looked over his shoulder and saw Markieff talking to Serenity. She seemed upset and he wondered what was going on. There was an explosion of applause from the crowd causing Lamont to turn around. Kian had the ball again and was running the field scoring another touchdown.

"What I miss?" Markieff asked, coming back.

"Your stepson is a fucking beast out here. Little dude going to be hell when he gets older. Shit, kind of remind me of your college days." Lamont joked.

SOUL Publications

"Cut it out," Markieff playfully bumped him. "Ugh, I just wish Mykel was out there. Him running the ball, Kian out here catching everything that comes his way, our team is unstoppable."

"Man, we are going undefeated this season," the other coach, Mark proudly yelled.

"You already know." Markieff and Lamont said in unison then laughed.

"Aye, I need a ride after the game." Markieff told Lamont.

"Where the fuck your car at nigga?"

"I let Serenity take it. She needed to get out of here. Plus, she wanted to go over to her parents and help set up for the cookout."

"Cookout. Can I come too?" Lamont asked.

Markieff shook his head and laughed. "Yea man, you can be my plus one. Greedy ass."

"You know a nigga love to eat." Lamont rubbed his stomach.

For the rest of the game, Kian scored two more touchdowns. Each time he did he looked up in the stands to Aaron, but his head was down in his phone. Once the game was over, Kian realized Serenity wasn't there.

"Hey, where my mother go?" Kian asked Markieff.

"She went over to your grandparent's house to help with the cookout."

"How she get there?"

"My car."

"Oh. So how you getting home?"

"You ask too many questions, but coach Lamont will bring me over to the cookout."

"Can I come with you?" Kian pouted.

Before Markieff could open his mouth to answer Kian, Aaron was calling for him.

"Ki, let's go." He yelled, with his head still down into his phone.

"I'm going with coach," Kian told him, without even getting an answer from Markieff.

That got Aaron's attention quick. His head popped up and he scowled at Kian. "Ki, I said let's go boy."

"Yo, you don't have to talk to him like that." Markieff scoffed, not liking Aaron's tone. He was sick of his attitude and was about to check him.

Lamont saw the steam coming out of Markieff ears and knew what time it was. He grabbed Markieff's arm. "Bruh, this not the place. Come on, kids out here."

Aaron handed Kian his phone and told him to get in the car. Kian snatched it and stormed off. Aaron stood in front of Markieff with a wide grin on his face.

"Listen, I don't know you but I smell the bullshit you coming with. Stay the fuck away from my family."

Markieff let out a snicker. "Your family. Nigga, staying away is something you know best. But like you said, you don't know me, but it's best you find out. I already let your little punk ass get fly out the mouth once and on behalf of these kids, you get another one. Now, I understand you feel threatened and it's cool, I would be too. Then again, if you were doing your job as a husband, you wouldn't feel the way you feel. Little friendly advice, take care of home before the next man does." With that, he patted Aaron's chest.

Aaron looked down at Markieff's hand and balled his fist to his side. He kissed his teeth and turned around to leave. "Bitch ass."

"Stop talking about yourself." Markieff said once he heard what Aaron called himself mumbling.

Getting in the car Aaron slammed his door shut. He was fuming with anger and wanted to punch Markieff dead in his face. He had never been tested like this and didn't know how to handle it.

"Eww, daddy what is this?" Kian asked, looking at something on his phone.

Aaron quickly snatched it from him. "Why are you in my phone Ki?" He fussed, trying to delete the picture that Nene just sent him of her nude with red pumps on.

"I was playing a game. Who was that lady?"

"I don't know. It had to be the wrong number." Aaron quickly lied.

"She nasty. She shouldn't send pictures like that to strangers."

"Yea, yea you right son. Aye listen, don't tell your mother about this. She will go crazy knowing you seen something like that."

Kian held out his hand and Aaron narrowed his eyes looking down at it then back at the road. "What you got your hand out for?"

"Well you know, 2k19 is about to drop and in case you're not home, I can just tell mommy to take me to GameStop to get it. I won't have to worry about her telling me to wait until you get home." Kian smiled.

"I can't believe I'm getting blackmailed by my damn son. You know what blackmail is?"

"Yea," Kian laughed.

Aaron shook his head. "I have to get cash. I will give it to you later."

"Ok."

Aaron stopped at the traffic light and checked the rest of his messages. Nene sent tons of photos and he quickly deleted them. He then sent her a message telling her not to text until he got back to her.

Pulling up to the house, he hated that he was stuck here for God knows how many hours. Before he could make a complete stop, Kian was out the car and took off to the house.

"I hope that damn boy don't tell," Aaron mumbled to himself. Walking into the house, he spotted Serenity talking to Treasure. She rolled her eyes at him before turning her back to him. He let out a frustrated breath of air, knowing this was going be a long day. He took out his phone and texted his brother to come over so he could have somebody to talk to.

Walking down the hall he was headed to the guest bathroom before he ran into Egypt. She turned her nose up at him giving him a look of disgust.

"Fuck you looking at me like that for?"

"You aint' shit, you know that?"

"Why, because I'm not fucking you anymore?" Aaron scoffed.

Egypt quickly looked back, making sure nobody was around to hear Aaron's comment. "That was a fucking mistake and I thought we wasn't going to speak about that shit. Just like you promised to never cheat on my sister again." She grunted.

"Yea well if your sister was doing her wifely duties, then maybe I wouldn't have to go elsewhere to get what I want."

"Then maybe you should leave her and stop all this bullshit. My sister deserves happiness."

"Just like she deserved happiness when you were sucking my dick," Aaron barked. "What, you mad you're not the side bitch now?"

Egypt lifted her hand and quickly smacked Aaron across the face. "Fuck you Aaron."

"You wish you could." He smirked rubbing the side of his face. "Now your ass standing here trying to have some type of morals and shit."

"I hope my sister leaves your dog ass. Just know karma is a bitch and she's going to pay your ass a visit. One day my sister is going see you for who you are and leave you hurting. At this point, I'm willing to risk it all and tell her everything

"Go ahead and watch how quick Darren is going to be done with your ass. Let's not forget about Benny. You think your father will be ok with your hoe ass fucking his favorite daughter's husband." Aaron smirked.

Instead of responding, Egypt pushed him out her way and stormed off. Aaron laughed to himself, baffled that she was really trying to check him for cheating when she was one of his women.

****

Outside Serenity was sitting at the table talking with Treasure, telling her what happened between her and Aaron.

"Girl, this nigga had the nerve to ask me, why was I still here once I told him he was cheating. Then at the game, he kept accusing me of fucking Markieff."

"Humph, that's because his ass guilty and trying to flip the script. See, at first I thought you probably was overthinking shit. Hearing how he been acting, girl his ass fucking somebody else. Fuck Aaron's black ass." Treasure grunted. She hated a cheater and furthermore hated seeing her friend hurt.

"I don't know what happened to us," Serenity sighed. She lowered her head and started playing with her ring. "He used to be so romantic. I remember the day we met. He came into my father's barbershop with his chocolate ass looking fine as ever. I had never seen him in there before that day. I couldn't keep my eyes off him. After that day, I never saw him again. Months later, when I got to Temple University there he was. We had the same English class. I tried to stop staring at him and couldn't. He noticed me looking and approached me. We walked down the street to grab something to eat. He had just moved to Philly from Maryland for school." Serenity paused and chuckled. "Not even two months later, I was pregnant with Kian. He was so damn happy. A year later, we got married. He begged me to be a stay at home wife but I wasn't built like that. Once Kian was old enough, my ass started working." She explained.

"Where do you think y'all went wrong?" Treasure asked.

Serenity shrugged her shoulders. "I have no clue. I thought it all started when he got his promotion at work, but thinking back, it seems like it was way before then. I just didn't see the signs."

"Don't blame yourself."

"Who else is there to blame? I must not be doing something right. Like, we lost our spark. I wanted the type of love my parents have. They been married forever. I'm sure my dad did his dirt, but my mother stuck by him. Me, I don't think I can if Aaron is really cheating. I mean if there is no trust, what's the point. I'm not about to sit around worrying what he's doing every time he walks out the door."

"Ma, I'm hungry." Kian said, running up to Serenity interrupting her conversation.

"Boy, what's wrong with your hands?" Serenity asked.

"Grandma said she didn't want my dirty ass hands digging in her food."

"Kian watch your mouth," Serenity popped him.

"What!" Kian shrugged his shoulders and giggled. "That's what she said and to tell you exactly like she said it," he explained.

Serenity had to giggle herself as she shook her head, knowing he wasn't lying. Her mother was petty and knew better than to tell him that. She got up and headed into the house.

"Girl, bring me back some of those cheesecake bites," Treasure yelled out.

"Greedy ass," Serenity laughed. Turning around to go into the house, she bumped into Markieff.

"I know you see this big body standing here. You just wanted to touch me, didn't you?" He joked.

"No," Serenity chuckled. She tried to step around him, but he moved in the same direction. She then stepped to her left and Markieff went the same direction as her. "Boy move," she hissed.

Markieff licked his lips. "Make me."

Serenity narrowed her eyes getting this funny vibe between them. She got nervous for some strange reason. The way Markieff stared at her had her feeling like a schoolgirl. She lowered her head to avoid the intense stare from Markieff. Markieff then placed his hand under her chin, making her look at him.

"You good shorty?" He curiously asked.

"Yea. I would like for you to get out my damn way," Serenity laughed.

"Ard, ard. I just wanted to make sure you was good. I'm about to go holla at Mr. B." Out of nowhere, Markieff leaned over and kissed her forehead.

Serenity couldn't help but blush as a chill ripped through her body. She opened the sliding door and stepped inside.

"What are you smiling so hard for?" Egypt asked, entering the kitchen from the other side.

"Humph, probably because her partner in crime is back around. Why you didn't tell me Markieff was home?" Her mother Kathy asked.

"Hold up, Markieff is back. Girl, let me go fix my makeup," Egypt said, running back to the bathroom.

Kathy shook her head. "That girl always had a crush on that boy. So, how is everything going with you baby girl?"

"It's cool." Serenity dryly answered.

"Umm hum," Kathy hummed. "Anytime you say it's cool, something is bothering you. So, tell mama what it is."

Serenity glanced out the door and into the backyard. She saw Markieff acting like a big kid, running away from Kian and a few of the other kids that were at the cookout. She felt bad for him, because she knew he was missing his own child. Thinking about something, she excused herself and went to make a phone call.

****

In the backyard, Markieff was hunched over trying to catch his breath. "Hold up y'all, I need a break," he said, between gasping for air.

"Damn, your ass needs to get in shape bruh," Lamont shook his head.

"Fuck you," Markieff laughed.

"Yo, who is that coming this way. She is cheesing like a mutherfucker." Lamont pointed out, seeing Egypt coming their way.

"Oh, that's Lucky's sister, Egypt." Markieff informed him.

"Mannn, why you call her Lucky?"

Markieff smiled from ear to ear thinking back to his younger days. "When I was a youngin, I used to hang around the old heads playing dice. My ass never would win and they had no problem taking my damn money. Serenity started chilling with me when I was out there and no lie, every time she was around I walked away with a fat pocket. No lie, when she would come around her pops would say here come your Lucky Charm, so I just started calling her that shit. She even got a tattoo of that shit on her upper leg." Markieff smiled, remembering the first time he saw her tattoo.

Egypt finally made it over to them. She rolled her eyes at Aaron who was standing close by. She then opened her arms wide going up to Markieff.

"Oh my God, Serenity didn't tell me you were back. How have you been?" She asked, wrapping her arms around him.

Markieff gave her a one arm pat on the back and stepped back. "I'm good. Just out here trying to make sure my son is good."

"Aww, you have a son? How old is he?" Egypt cooed.

"He's twelve. Matter fact, he and Kian are cool."

"Ok ok. Wow, you're looking good." Egypt smiled, lusting all over him.

Moments later, Benny called Markieff's name and waved him over.

"Good seeing you Egypt," Markieff said, walking off before she could get a word in. He walked up to Benny with opened arms. "Mr. B, long time old man."

"Who you calling old youngin? Shit, I may be sixty but I look better then half these young bulls around here." Benny beamed with pride.

"No lie, old head does look good for his age," Lamont complimented.

"Mont, don't boost his head up." Markieff joked.

For a good twenty minutes they joked back and forth along with catching up.

"I know you're just coming back, but how do you feel about taking over for me?" Benny asked.

"Honestly, once I got settled I was coming to see you. I got a regular gig to hold me over until I caught up with you."

"Good. Because I'm ready to give this shit up. I want to stay my black ass home. I would have given it to Serenity, but I don't want Aaron nowhere near my business. He works for a company that could make a lot of money from me and I'm not selling out like that."

Markieff just nodded his head understanding where Benny was coming from. Benny was the business owner of a lot of properties around Philly and been doing things on his own for a long time. He extended his hand towards Benny and said, "I'm in. No need for my business degree to go to waste," Markieff chuckled.

"What type of work you're doing now?" Benny asked.

"Well, I'm a security guard down at the bank Serenity works at. It's been hard trying to find something in my field and security was a easy gig to get."

"Look like they about to be a man short," Benny joked.

For the rest of the cookout they finished catching up. But once the crowd died down they started a game of dice.

"Hey, where is your Lucky Charm?" Benny halfway joked.

"Good question," Markieff said, looking around. When he spotted her a wide grin painted his face.

"Daddy," Mykel yelled, running over to Markieff. He hugged his leg and looked up at him. "You said you wasn't leaving me again. Why you didn't come get me for my game?"

Markieff let out a frustrated breath of air. He knew Shana probably lied to Mykel and he wasn't going to tell Mykel the truth about his mother.

"Dad, it's ok. Ms. Serenity said I can't tell mommy I was with you."

Markieff got down on one knee. "She's right baby boy, you can't. Look, your mommy mad at me right now and... We just can't let her know until I get this worked out. So on the weekends Ms. Serenity's going to get you and bring you to my house."

"Ok, I like that." Mykel smiled. "Now can I got play with Kian?"

"Yea, go ahead. He's in the house."

Looking over to Serenity Markieff mouthed, "Thank you."

She blew him a kiss, causing his smile to widen.

Lamont elbowed Markieff getting his attention. "Bruh, look at all that ass," he said, watching Egypt bending over to pick something up. They then watched as she walked off.

"Man, that shit paid for. I like my women to be naturally thick, like my Lucky Charm."

"Your Lucky Charm huh?" Lamont leaned closer and whispered in Markieff's ear. "You know her husband behind us?"

"And. That nigga know Serenity thick as hell. Curves in all the right places. I mean think about this. You hitting it from the back and squeezing that ass and all of a sudden, shit deflate like a balloon. Don't have to worry about that shit when fucking a woman like Lucky," Markieff added knowing Aaron's ears was wide open.

Aaron heard enough and walked around standing in front of Markieff. "You got one more time to mention my fucking wife," he grunted.

"Mont, Lucky got some juicy ass lips too." Markieff tilted his head looking Aaron dead in his face. Just as Aaron opened his mouth to say something, Markieff's fist was driving into his face. He then hit him with a upper cut underneath his chin lifting him off his feet.

Aaron quickly gathered himself jumping back to his feet. He charged at Markieff swinging his fists wildly. He managed to tap the side of Markieff's face, but it wasn't enough to even move him. Markieff countered back and jabbed Aaron in his midsection followed by another uppercut. Aaron went back down on the ground, not able to hold his balance.

Lamont quickly grabbed Markieff before he could do anything else. It was still a few people left and he didn't need Markieff making a big scene. Benny walked over and grabbed Markieff's arm pretending to be mad.

"How dare you come into my home acting like some thug," Benny fussed. He then whispered, "Thank you. That square ass nigga needed to be touched."

Serenity looked down at Aaron and knew he was embarrassed. She walked over to Aaron to help him up, he knocked her hand out the way.

"Fuck out my way," Aaron scowled getting up.

Lamont was still there and stepped in front of Aaron once he was up.

"Yo, she was just trying to help your dumb ass. Disrespect her again and I will send your dumbass back down there."

Serenity quickly stepped in between the two, pushing Lamont back. "Mont, it's cool."

Finally hours later, Aaron's brother James arrived. James took a second and looked around. "Damn, party over already?"

Aaron bumped his shoulder into Lamont as he walked over to James. "Yea, let's go. I need a ride home."

"Nigga, you going to need a ride to the hospital." Lamont yelled as he started to follow behind Aaron.

"Mont, let him go." Serenity begged.

James stood there for a second eyeing Lamont.

"Jay, please get your brother out of here. Tell him I will be home later, so we can talk." Serenity told him.

James nodded his head and jogged behind Aaron. Serenity shamefully looked around the back yard seeing the few people left whispering and staring. She then went into the house to check on Markieff. He wasn't in the living room or kitchen. She could hear Markieff and her father's voice and went down the hall to Benny's home office. She opened the door causing both of them to turn in her direction.

"I will leave you two to talk." Benny said walking out.

Once Benny was gone, Serenity went over to Markieff.

"Oh my God, I'm so sorry about Aaron. Are you ok?" Serenity asked out of concern.

Markieff kissed his teeth. "Why wouldn't I be? I'm sorry, but your husband hit's like a fucking bitch."

Serenity wanted to laugh but held it in.

"You know damn well you want to laugh," Markieff joked. "But yo, I'm ready to slide. You coming over to the house to chill with us for a little?" He changed up the subject.

"I guess, since Mykel is with me." Serenity answered with a slight chuckle.

They both walked out the office and gathered their things. Serenity handed Markieff her car keys and made him drive back to his place. When they got there, Kian and Mykel jumped out the car and ran to the house, waiting for Markieff to come unlock the door.

"Hurry up daddy, Fortnite is waiting for us," Mykel impatiently stated.

"Boy, calm your nerves, I'm coming." Markieff shot back.

Soon as Markieff had the door unlocked and opened, the boys took off upstairs. Markieff shook his head and went straight to the kitchen. Serenity kicked off her shoes and flopped down on his couch. Moments later, Markieff came back with two glasses and a bottle of beer for him and Tequila.

"You ready to get fucked up?"

"Umm, I don't think so. I still have to drive home." Serenity replied.

"Your ass not going home, so get ready to turn up." Markieff poured some Tequila and done the same with Serenity's cup. "Let me ask you this, what the fuck are you doing with this punk ass nigga? His tight jean wearing ass don't seem like your type."

"Boy, you don't even know what my type is. Aaron was a good man when we hooked up in college."

"Was?" Markieff guzzled down his drink giving Serenity the side eye. He knew it was something behind how she said was.

Serenity followed suit and took her shot to the head and poured herself another shot, wishing she worded her comment differently.

"Watch out Ms. I have to drive home. Top me off."

"Excuse me?" Serenity scoffed.

Markieff shook his head, realizing his words came out wrong. "Get your head out the gutter. I'm talking about another shot," he raised his glass.

"I knew that." Serenity said, playing it off.

"So, he playing you?"

Serenity let out a sigh. "Don't mention this to my dad, but yea...well. I don't know for sure, but his actions speak volumes."

"Nah, trust that gut feeling you got shorty. Don't ignore that shit."

Serenity took her shot to the head and allowed what Markieff said sink in. Markieff placed his glass on the table and grabbed his beer. He drunk a little of it and placed it on the table. He then reached down grabbing Serenity's legs and placing them on his lap.

"What are you doing?" She asked, trying to pull away.

"Chill girl." He took her feet into his hands and started rubbing them. "You remember this?"

A smile crept along Serenity's face. When they was younger, Markieff would always rub her feet as they chilled watching movies.

"Yea, I remember. Your ass had a foot fetish."

"I wouldn't say it was a damn fetish. Matter fact, you got these dogs done," Markieff joked, pulling off her socks.

"Ugh, you play so much." She kicked him with a smirk on her face.

"You like it. I see you still got some pretty feet."

"Umm hmm, foot fetish like I said."

"Whatever. But for real Lucky, what's up with this nigga Aaron?"

"I don't want to talk about him. You know what, Kian come on," Serenity yelled. "I need to get home."

"Bullshit. You're not going anywhere and if that nigga have a problem with it, he can come pick you up. I'm not letting you drive home."

Kian came downstairs with a frown on his face. "Why I can't stay the night with Mykel and Uncle Markieff?"

"You are. Tell Mykel to give you a pair of his shorts and a t-shirt to sleep in." Markieff answered.

Kian looked over to Serenity for conformation.

She rolled her eyes. "Bye Ki."

"Yes," Kian cheered. "Kel, I'm staying." He took off running.

Markieff smiled and stood to his feet. "I'm going to take a shower, you want to join me?"

"You full of jokes tonight. You know damn well I'm not joining your ass."

Markieff shrugged his shoulders with a smirk on his face. "I didn't know that."

Serenity shook her head watching him jog up the stairs. Sitting back in the chair she got comfortable and pulled out her phone. She then logged onto her Facebook page to see what was going on down her timeline. She then typed in Markieff's name and pulled up his page. Her lips curved into a smile once she saw his profile picture. He was shirtless, flexing his muscles after working out. Her tongue then ran across her lips as she admired the picture. Seconds later, she quickly exited off his page.

"No, no, no. Why am I feeling this way? This is your boy, the homie. Serenity, get it together you're still married," she lectured herself. "Stop lusting over this man, you're a married woman." She looked up at the picture of Markieff hanging on his wall and couldn't ignore the feeling she was getting, even if she wanted to.

Chapter 6

Aaron stood at the front door of the last place he needed to be. He knocked and took a step back, waiting for the person to come to the door. When he didn't get a response the first time, his knocks slowly turned into banging as he yelled.

"Egypt, come open this damn door."

Moments later, the door swung open and Egypt stepped out, closing her door behind her.

"What the fuck are you doing here?" She asked sternly, just above a whisper.

"Let me in."

"Boy, are you crazy? Why would I fucking do that?"

"Because you need that fucking job, right? I don't feel like staying at a hotel, so open the damn door and let me in before I fire your ass."

"Fuck you and that damn job. Now get the fuck on." Egypt snarled. She went back into the house and slammed the door in his face.

"E, stop fucking playing man. Open this damn door." Aaron continued to yell.

Egypt opened the door and rolled her eyes. She gave in and stepped to the side letting him in. Not even stopping in the living room, he went straight to her bedroom.

"Where is Darren?" He asked, plopping down on her bed.

"Minding his business. Why are you here Aaron? Shouldn't you be home with your wife?"

Aaron sucked his teeth. "Man, fuck her."

Getting closer to him, Egypt noticed the bruises on his face. "Who beat your ass?" She left the cookout and didn't see when Markieff Mayweather Aaron's ass.

"That nigga didn't beat my ass. He got me from behind." Aaron lied.

"Whatever. Again, why are you here like you didn't curse me out a few hours ago."

"I need some information. What's up with this Markieff nigga? He been getting fly at the mouth at the cookout and...and I see the way Serenity looks at him. They got history or something?"

"Oh, I see. That bitch Karma came a little early." Egypt sat down on her bed crossing her legs. "Yea, they used to be together when they were teenagers. When Markieff moved away they lost contact with each other. He was her first love and honestly, they only broke up because he moved. It's not like it's bad blood between them." Egypt smiled, knowing her lies was eating Aaron up.

"So, he's not a friend of the family?" Aaron asked.

"Nope. Well, yea he is. He and my father were close, all thanks to Serenity. His Lucky Charm."

Aaron chuckled to himself and got up. He rubbed the back of his head unsure of how to feel about what Egypt told him. He stared at Egypt for a second then started to walk out the room. As something came to his mind, he stopped and turned around.

"You're lying like a muterfucker. I just thought about something, I was Serenity's first. Even before we got together in college, she said she only had one boyfriend and his name was Jeffery. She said it was back in her senior year of high school and that shit wasn't that deep."

"Ok, don't believe me." Egypt got up and walked to her door. "Your time is up."

Aaron chuckled. He kissed Egypt's cheek. "You funny as hell girl. I see what you just tried to do. Throwing shade, thinking I'm going to get mad at your sister and be back in your bed? Not going to work." Aaron threw up his two fingers saying, "I'm gone."

Once he got in his car, he couldn't help but give what Egypt said some thought. Serenity could have lied to him about him being her first. Just as quick as that thought came to his mind, he pushed it out. That was a lifetime ago and furthermore, they were teenagers. He wasn't about to sweat a teenage love affair.

Pulling up to the driveway, he was surprised when he didn't see Serenity's car parked in the driveway. Taking out his phone, he called her to see where she was this late with Kian.

"Yes Aaron?" Serenity answered, sounding irritated.

"Where the hell you at?"

"Why." Serenity dryly answered.

"The fuck you mean why? Where is Kian?"

"He's with me. I have to go, so see you in the morning." Serenity quickly said before ending the call.

Aaron pulled the phone from his ear and blankly stared at it. "Did she just hang up on me?"

****

Back at Markieff's house, Markieff looked at Serenity warily.

"What?" Serenity said, placing her phone on the coffee table and grabbing her drink.

"You should have told him you was chilling with a real nigga."

"And his ass would have had a temper tantrum. I don't feel like going back and forth with him right now."

"Temper tantrum? Just say that nigga was going to act like a little bitch."

Serenity took a pillow and playfully hit him. "Anyways, you know tomorrow is Sunday and my parents still have dinner at the house. You should come." She said, changing up the subject.

"Word, I'm in there. I used to love having dinner at y'all house."

Changing the subject again, Serenity asked, "Why do men cheat?"

"Because they can. A man only does what a woman allows."

"That's bullshit. What a woman allows? So, you're telling me if I knew a man was cheating on me, I would let him?"

"Shit, you doing it now." Markieff bluntly answered.

"Really, that's how you feel?"

"Lucky, I'm just keeping it real with you. You see the signs and you're ignoring them. Therefore, his ass is going to do what you allow him to do. Let me ask you this, have you ever questioned him about his bullshit?"

"I did, and he denied it." Serenity quickly answered.

"Of course he did." Markieff chuckled. He stood to his feet and extended his hand to help Serenity up. "Come with me, I got something you need to relax a little more."

Serenity gave Markieff the side eye.

"Girl, get your ass up and come with me."

Serenity rolled her eyes as she got up and followed him into the backyard. She sat across from him at the patio table. Markieff then pulled out a blunt and some weed.

"Really, we about to smoke?"

"Hell yea," Markieff smiled. "Your ass used to be the first one to roll up and zone the hell out."

"I haven't smoked in years. Aaron said it wasn't lady like."

Markieff kissed his teeth. "Fuck that nigga."

Serenity eased back into her chair and watched as Markieff rolled up the blunt. She grabbed his beer and took a sip.

"Yo, what you doing? I don't know where your lips been." Markieff joked.

"Oh shut up. We about to smoke together so clearly you don't care where they been."

"You got that one," he laughed. He was done and placed the blunt to his lips and fired it up. He pulled on it hard before passing it to Serenity.

Serenity slowly took in the smoke, allowing it to do its job of relaxing her.

"Feeling good I see." Markieff pointed out.

Serenity didn't comment right away. She took another puff and passed it back to Markieff. For a moment she sat silently. For at least five minutes they sat in silence.

"Is it me?" Serenity blurted out, breaking the silence.

"Is what you?"

"Is it something I did to make him cheat?"

"Yo, don't blow my high worrying about that tight, stick up the ass, fake ass gangster in a suit wearing jackass."

Serenity couldn't help but burst out in laughter. "Really, all that?"

"Hell yea."

Instead of responding to what Markieff said, Serenity closed her eyes and relaxed like she was supposed to. She was glad Markieff was back in her life. Although it's been years since they saw each other, it felt like they never missed a beat. Titling her head, she looked over to him and smiled. She could only wonder what life could have been like if he never moved away.

"Take a picture, it lasts longer," Markieff said, feeling her eyes on him.

"Boy, shut up." Was all Serenity could say caught red handed staring.

"What happened between you and Shana?"

"I guess I wasn't enough for her. She left me for a nigga she thought was going to the NBA. But when bull turned out to be a bigger hoe than she was, she dipped. By that time, I had moved on. No lie, I was still fucking her on and off. I really loved her, but realized I was holding myself back from finding real love still dealing with her. I thought I had found the one a few years back. Shorty was everything I was looking for in a woman. But like a man, I was thinking with my little head and fucked up everything. Shana set me up. She came over one night and we fucked. What I didn't know is she was recording us and showed my girl. Next thing I know, she moved on with the next nigga and took Mykel." Markieff explained.

"Well damn. Her ass told us her son's father was killed. I can't believe she done you like that."

"Me either. But next subject." Markieff suggested, not in the mood to talk about his past with Shana. It was still a painful memory he was trying to get over.

Serenity let out a big yawn as she stretched her arms. "I think we talked enough. I'm getting sleepy. How about we call it a night and get some sleep."

"Ard. I have a guest room you can crash in." Markieff stood up and took Serenity to the guest room. "Bathroom down the hall. I will go get you one of my shirts and shorts to sleep in."

"Thank you." Serenity smiled. Serenity walked down to the bathroom and started her shower.

Markieff stood in the doorway getting her attention. "Here you go," he said, handing Serenity the clothes.

Serenity took them and pushed him out the way, closing the door. She hurried and took her shower. Going back to the room, she flopped down on the bed and it didn't take long for her to fall off to sleep.

The next day, it was around noon when Serenity woke up. She could hear yelling coming from the living room. Getting up, she went into the bathroom to use it and then off to the living room to see what was going on.

"Uncle Markieff, you suck in 2k. I told you, you couldn't beat me. And you better pay up," she heard Kian yelling.

"Kian, watch your mouth." Serenity warned him. She sat down in the recliner and watched as they played the game.

"It's cool Lucky," Markieff ensured her. "I made lunch. Yours is in the microwave."

"You didn't have to do that."

"I know. Just shut up and go eat."

Serenity shook her head. She headed to the kitchen for her food because her stomach was growling. Opening the microwave, she saw it was plate of eggs and rice with a few slices of bologna. She closed the microwave and warmed her plate. Markieff came into the kitchen and sat down at the table.

"I see you have a good memory. I haven't had eggs and rice in so long." Serenity smiled.

"Yea, I bet you haven't. I know that was one of our favorites. Shit, that was the only thing Benny would fix us when your moms was gone."

"Speaking of my mother, let me call her. I'm usually at the house already helping her start dinner. I know she's going to curse my ass out."

"Hell yea. She already called Kian's phone fussing." Markieff smirked.

"And you didn't come wake me up?"

"See, I was but you looked so peaceful as you slept. I didn't want to wake you."

"Umm hmm, you just like hearing my mother fuss." Serenity playfully rolled her eyes.

"That too." Markieff laughed.

Kian came into the kitchen with his phone in his hand. "Ma, dad keeps calling me. He texted and asked where we were. I didn't answer him because I didn't know what to tell him."

"That's fine baby. I will talk to him later. Go change, we are about to go so we can head over to your grandparents house for dinner."

"Ugh, do I have to? Can I just stay here?"

"No, Mykel is coming with us too and Uncle Markieff will meet us there."

"Yes," Kian excitedly yelled and took off to tell Mykel the good news.

"Well, being that me and Mont play ball on Sunday, I'm bringing him with me, if that's cool?"

"Yea, you can. Matter fact, I will call up Treasure. That girl swears she doesn't like him, but I can tell she does. She's been dealing with so much with her ex, she's guarded. I know Lamont cool people and may be what she needs."

"Look at you, trying to be a matchmaker."

"I try," Serenity laughed. "Let me get out of here so I can run home and change my clothes."

"Ard, see you later."

Serenity went to the room and put on her clothes from the night before. The boys were downstairs waiting for her. When she got in the car, she called her mother, knowing she was about to hear an earful.

"Humph, I see you're finally up." Kathy scoffed.

"I know Ma, I had a long night. Me and Markieff was up all night catching up. I'm headed home to change clothes and will be over there shortly."

"Oh, you stayed the night with him?"

"Long story and we can talk about it when I get there. I'm pulling in my driveway now."

"Ok, but don't rush. Your Aunt Thresa and cousin Shanita are here helping me. So, almost everything is done. Make sure you invite Markieff over. I remember how that boy loves my food."

"I did. Well, see you in a little." Serenity rolled her eyes seeing Aaron coming out the house, doing something he does best, leaving. Serenity didn't even say anything to him as she walked into the house.

"Well, hello to you too?" Aaron hissed.

"Hey," Serenity dryly spoke.

"Hey dad," Kian said, running by giving Aaron a high five.

Aaron gave Kian and Mykel high fives as they passed. "At least somebody happy to see me."

"Damn sure ain't me," Serenity mumbled.

"What you say?" Aaron asked.

"Nothing. Are you coming to eat dinner at my parents?"

"Don't I always come?"

"Whatever," Serenity waved her hands. She noticed the black eye Aaron was sporting and wanted to laugh, but kept it in. When she got into the house, she let it out. Her phone started to ring and she quickly answered it seeing it was Egypt calling.

"Girl, where are you?" Egypt hissed into the phone.

"I'm just getting home to change clothes. I will be there in twenty minutes.

"Please, hurry up. Shanita is over here and you know I can't stand that bitch."

"Humph, that used to be your favorite cousin. Shit, at one point I thought you liked her ass more than me," Serenity joked.

"Ugh, whatever heffa. But yea, once upon a time."

"You know, you never told me what the hell happened between y'all. Shit, I can't even remember the last time I saw her or Auntie."

"Just know, her ass ain't shit and she not loyal. Now, get off the phone and hurry up and get here."

"I'm coming now."

Serenity ended the call and her little mind went to wondering what possibly could have caused her sister and cousin to really fall out. At first, Serenity didn't care but now she was curious. On her way out the house she texted Treasure telling her to come over and join the family for dinner.

Chapter 7

Before going to dinner Aaron stopped by his brother James' house. James had a few of their friends over watching the Eagles football game. Aaron's eyes was on the television, but he wasn't watching the game. His mind was on overload and that game was the furthest thing from his mind. He took a sip of his beer thinking about the threat Nene made earlier that morning. She told him if he didn't make his decision soon, she was going to tell Serenity herself about their affair.

"Bruh, you good?" James asked, waving his hand in front of Aaron.

Aaron shook his head snapping out of his daze then answered James. "Hell nah, I'm not good. Nene ass yelling she going to tell Serenity everything."

James disappointedly shook his head and pointed his finger in Aaron's face. "See, that's what your ass gets. I told you to leave that crazy bitch alone. I understand y'all had history before you and Serenity, but you should have left that bitch alone. Riddle me this little bruh, why the fuck did you marry Serenity if your stupid ass still had plans to fuck with Nene? I don't get that shit."

"Don't get me wrong I loved Serenity, but, she stopped doing the things that made me fall in love with her. Like, we grew apart and only sticking around for Kian."

"That's a bunch of bullshit." James said frustrated. "Sticking around is doing more damage than you think. Keep it up and you're going to find yourself hurt just as much as Serenity when shit hits the fan. Nene threatening to out y'all, and that bitch just might do it. Oh, let's not forget the fact that you fucked your sister in law too. Don't think that shit not going to leak too."

Aaron took a big sip of his beer allowing James' words to playback into his head. He knew what he was saying was nothing but the truth. He knew Kian shouldn't have been the reason he stayed, but he really didn't know why he did. At one point he did love Serenity and couldn't see himself without her in his life. Yes, he and Nene once had a relationship, but he found out that Nene wasn't everything she claimed to be. He was new to the city, so he didn't know everything about her before falling hard for her. When they broke up, he was truly heartbroken. That's when he found Serenity and something about her reminded him of Nene. Years later, he and Nene ran into each other and been messing around on and off since. Breaking his thoughts was their friend Calvin as he broke his silence.

"Jay let me ask you, if you was married, you wouldn't cheat?" Calvin inquired.

"No, I wouldn't because of the fact I watched my mother cry many nights wondering where my father was. I told myself I wouldn't do the shit that man did. And for my brother to be doing the same shit is pissing me off. Furthermore, if I had a good woman at home why would I step out on her?"

Calvin sucked his teeth. "Nigga, whatever. Go somewhere with that high and mighty shit. Aaron, if Serenity not onto your shit, just keep Nene happy and do you. Shit, why fuck up a good thing?"

"Aaron, don't listen to that fool." James scoffed.

"What? I'm just saying, if he been getting away with the shit he just need to tighten up and keep Nene happy so she won't tell shit."

"See, that's the thing. I think I fucked up, because the other day Serenity mentioned something about cheating. I played that shit off and changed up the argument. But, I gotta get Nene under control." Aaron said.

"So, what are you going to do?" James asked.

"What I always do. Eat her pussy good, throw some money her way and stay a weekend with her. Shit should buy me some time." Aaron shrugged his shoulders.

"Stupid, that's all I'm going to say. Don't come here when this little plan of yours blows up in your face." James advised him. James was about to leave the conversation alone, but had to give his brother something else to think about. "You know what your problem is, you're just like daddy. You want the best of both worlds. You want your cake and eat it too."

"You know, I never understood that shit. I mean when you get cake, you're supposed to eat that shit," Aaron joked.

"Nigga, you're missing the fucking point." James yelled in a stern tone. "You got Serenity at home doing everything she's supposed to as a wife. When your ass goes home you have a clean house, meal on the table. Serenity takes care of home. Nene takes care of your needs, I get that. So, why not just tell Serenity what she needs to do to take care of your needs and leave Nene ass alone for good, or just leave Serenity."

Aaron nodded his head up and down and knew what he had to do. He loved Serenity, but they got married way too early and he thought love would have brought them closer. For a while it did until temptation presented itself. He was weak and didn't know how to say no to the desires that came when it came to being with Egypt and Nene. He guessed Serenity got too comfortable and forgot to keep him satisfied. Well, that's at least what he was telling himself to justify his cheating.

When Aaron pulled up to the house, he let out a sigh seeing all the cars in the driveway. He hated coming to these Sunday dinners.

"Daddy, come play catch with me and Mykel," Kian said running towards the car.

Aaron got out the car. "Ard, I will meet you two in the backyard. Let me go tell your mother I'm here.

"Ok."

Just as Aaron was about to walk towards the house, a car pulled up. Something told him to keep walking but he stopped to see who occupied the car. His jaws clenched once he saw it was Markieff. Kian and Mykel was still on the porch when they saw Markieff getting out the car.

"Yes, coach you're here. Come on to the backyard so we can play catch. Hey dad, you don't have to come now." Kian informed him.

Lamont got out the car and wanted to laugh so bad. He peeped the anger written all over Aaron's face when Kian picked Markieff over him to play catch. Aaron mugged them as he walked inside the house.

"Bruh, he was big mad." Lamont joked.

"Fuck him," Markieff laughed.

When they walked inside they saw Aaron had found Serenity. Her face was frowned up as she followed behind him going upstairs.

"Somebody in trouble," Markieff said loud enough for both Aaron and Serenity to hear.

Aaron give him a scowl while Serenity laughed, throwing up her middle finger.

Once upstairs and away from the family, Aaron pushed Serenity into her old bedroom and slammed the door.

"What the fuck is wrong with you?" Serenity scoffed.

"Why is that nigga here?"

"Umm, to eat dinner." Serenity sarcastically stated.

"Don't play with me. This is a family dinner. This nigga not family?"

"Newsflash, he is. He's like the son my father never had. So, rather you like it or not he is family, so you will have to get used to him being around."

"Word, that's how you feel? What if I take you to my mother's house and one of my ex-girlfriends popped up out of the blue and started hanging around and shit? You wouldn't like that shit would you?"

"First off, Markieff is not a ex. Second, he's been a part of this family before you. So, if your mother happened to have had a special relationship with this person, I could care less. Unless your ass give me reason to think otherwise. What I don't understand is why you're so fucking threatened by Markieff."

Aaron sucked his teeth. "Don't play me like that. I'm not threatened by that man. I just don't like how he be looking at you and shit."

"Ok and?"

"What the fuck you mean ok and? You checking for this nigga or something."

Serenity let out a chuckle. "I'm not doing this with you. I can't believe you even questioning me about this shit when you got some shit going on with you." She went to walk away but Aaron quickly grabbed her arm.

"What is that supposed to mean. This your second time accusing me of something. Just come out and say what's on your mind."

Serenity placed her hands on her hips and got in Aaron's face, looking him dead in his eyes. "Are you or have you ever cheated on me?"

Aaron grabbed her by the waist and wrapped his arms around her. "No. I never cheated on you," he lied to her face.

"Then why the distance?" Serenity sighed.

"What distance?" Aaron asked, playing on her emotions. He was going to use this to make sure from here on out he covered his tracks, and kept Serenity at bay from his extra activities.

"For one, we haven't fucked in God knows when. Two, you're never home and I don't know, shit just seems different between us." Serenity sincerely expressed.

Aaron leaned closer and kissed her lips. "First, let me apologize for making you feel that way. Second, like you said this promotion been keeping me busy like crazy. I know it's been awhile, but you have to admit by the time I get home, you don't want me touching you. So really, you're to blame for the drought down there," he said, rubbing her between her legs.

Serenity quickly smacked his hand down. "Don't play with me. If you haven't been fucking me who's been satisfying your needs?"

Aaron stepped back and held up his hands. "My right and left with a whole lot of Pornhub." Aaron smirked, hoping this was enough to get Serenity off his back.

"Umm hmm, better be." Serenity hummed. She wasn't buying his sob story, but again she didn't have the proof to support what she thought she knew. She was going to keep an close eye on him. She didn't want to be wrong and just throw away her marriage off a feeling she had.

"Sooo, are we good?" Aaron asked with a smirk, trying to make her laugh.

"Long as you stop this insecure shit with Markieff. He is my friend and I would love for y'all to get along."

Aaron sucked his teeth not liking this, but he was going to agree to it to keep the peace with Serenity. "Yea, I guess. But tell his ass your name is Serenity, not some fucking Lucky Charm."

"Aww, you sound jelly. That's my nickname. Nothing to worry about." Serenity kissed his lips. "Now, come on so we can go eat," Serenity grabbed his hand.

Soon as they got back downstairs, Serenity spotted Shanita talking to Markieff and Lamont.

When Serenity first got to the house, Shanita had to make a run so she didn't see her. Shanita spotted Serenity coming down the stairs and stood to her feet.

"There goes my beautiful cousin. How have you been Serenity?" Shanita greeted her.

"Long time no see or hear Shanita." Serenity said, walking over giving her a hug.

"It has been a long time."

"Aaron, you remember my cousin Shanita?"

"Yea, I do. Nice to see you," Aaron extended his hand for a handshake. He then turned to Serenity and kissed her cheek. "Bae, I'm going to let you catch up with your cousin, I'm out back with Kian."

"Aww, I love black love. You two been together since what, college?" Shanita asked.

"Yes ma'am, Serenity beamed with pride.

"Glad to see you two still going strong."

Egypt walked into the living room and sucked her teeth loud enough for everyone to hear. Serenity gave her a knowing look, telling her to chill. Egypt just rolled her eyes and turned around going back out the room.

"Ugh, I don't know why your sister still acting like that towards me. We used to be so close." Shanita said. Funny thing about it, Shanita did know why but she couldn't tell Serenity. She knew about Egypt and Aaron and didn't want to be the one to tell her that her sister is a hoe and her husband is whore.

"Yea, y'all was. Hell, I'm curious to know what happened between y'all." Serenity pointed out. "But, let's not dwell on that. I'm glad you're here and maybe we all can work on getting back close."

"I would love that." Shanita said. I got a new job and will have so much more free time."

"Great. We can work on you and Egypt later."

"Don't hurt to try." Shanita smiled. She then looked over to Markieff and smiled. Turning back to Serenity, she leaned in closer and whispered something in her ear. "Girl, I see Markieff is still fine as hell. Is he single?"

"He is."

"Good, because his ass damn sure can get it. Shit, if he tell me to bend over I will say, yes daddy."

Serenity laughed and hit Shanita's shoulder. "Girl, I see nothing changed with you. You're still silly as hell."

"Serenity, can I talk to you for a second?" Egypt asked walking into the living room and headed for the front door.

Serenity excused herself and went outside with Egypt. Soon as Serenity stepped out the door, Egypt went off.

"Why you in there all buddy buddy with that bitch?"

"Wow, sooo, I can't talk to my own cousin?"

"No, because she's the enemy. When I beef with a bitch, you beef with a bitch, that's law."

Serenity crossed her arms over her chest. "Oh really? Well, since you put it like that, tell me why you beefing with Shanita."

"It shouldn't matter why."

"Ok for real, what happened between you two?"

"You know what, forget it. Do you Ren. Be friends with that bitch," Egypt stormed off and headed to her car.

"Where are you going? We haven't had dinner yet."

"I can't be here right now." Egypt said.

The front door opened and Markieff came out. He watched as Egypt sped out the driveway and down the street.

"What's up with you two?" Markieff asked.

Serenity shrugged her shoulders up and down. "Man, I don't fucking know. She tripping because I was talking to Shanita."

"Really? I thought y'all was tight? If memory serves me correct, those two used to be so close back in the day. What happened between them?"

"Who's knows. Egypt just being her usual self, the drama queen.

The front door came open and Aaron came walking out. He looked Markieff up and down before turning his attention to Serenity. "Bae, I gotta jet."

"Really?" Serenity scoffed.

"Don't act like this right now. James just called me about this account we need to go over. One of our clients sent an email about something that needs to be addressed before our meeting tomorrow. Look, I will make it up to you tonight when you get home." He kissed her cheek and jogged off.

Markieff's brows raised. Something wasn't right, but he wasn't going to say anything. But it was kind of odd that Egypt left first and now Aaron with his bullshit excuse to leave. He looked over to Serenity and wondered if she picked up on what he was thinking, because she stood for a second in a daze. As much as he wanted to put her on point, he didn't want to be the one to bring that situation to her with no proof.

"Come on Lucky, let's go eat." He said instead, placing his arm around her shoulders.

*****

Aaron wasn't lying about having to handle work. He was sitting in his office trying to figure things out with his account and with Nene. She been texting him and he has yet to answer her. He thought he had his mind made up but now, he wasn't sure what to do. Just like a man, losing Serenity never crossed his mind because he thought he was slick enough not to get caught. Sitting back in his chair he let out a frustrated breath of air. When he closed his eyes, Serenity's face popped in his head. She was smiling from ear to ear, but she was smiling at Markieff. It pissed Aaron off seeing how happy she gets when he was around. Even the way Kian took to Markieff had him in his feelings.

"Aaron, I think I got it," James said, knocking him out of his thoughts.

Aaron's eyes popped open and he sat up, pushing his chair closer to his desk. "Yea, what you got?"

James laid out the papers on Aaron's desk and showed him where the mistakes were. He then put in the right numbers, showing Aaron what the clients would like and would possibly be good enough to sign with their firm.

"Good catch," Aaron congratulated James' work.

"Now, what's up with you? Your ass been in here daydreaming, what's on your mind?"

"Life."

"Shit, don't think too hard, you might kill the last of your brain cells," James joked.

"Fuck you bruh," Aaron laughed. He then got up and started pacing back and forth. "Yo, you think it's possible to love two people at the same time?"

James shook his head. "Bruh, I thought we talked about this. You said you letting Nene crazy ass go."

"I was man...Man, I don't fucking know. Why this shit gotta be so damn complicated."

"It's complicated because you made it that way nigga." James snickered, disappointed in his brother's decisions.

"I know, I know... I never meant for it to get this deep."

"No, your ass never meant to get caught up. Dude, you been fucking with Nene for a while." James pointed out.

"Yea, but that's been on and off."

"Nigga, it doesn't matter if it was on and off, the shit still happened. Oh, let's not forget you fucked your sister in law."

"Don't remind me. At one point, I just knew for sure Serenity was going to catch us, but for a whole month we were able to do our thing."

"What happened with that? Why y'all stop?" James inquired.

Aaron shrugged his shoulders. "I don't know. She just stopped calling for the dick, and while we were at work we only talked business. I never asked her why and she never said shit about it, so I left well enough alone. We just agreed to never bring the shit up."

"So, why can't you leave Nene alone?"

"I don't know. Every time I think I'm done with her ass, I go back. It's like she got a fucking hold on me bruh."

"Yea, it's called pussy. The fact that your shit hasn't caught up with you, you go back. Sooner or later karma is going to pay that ass a visit. Fuck around and the shoe going to be on the other foot."

Aaron sucked his teeth. "Man please, Serenity's not the cheating type. Plus, she's not going anywhere."

"You really think if Serenity found out about your cheating ass she's going to stick around?"

"Yes. We will work that shit out, no doubt." Aaron said with confidence.

James crossed his arms over his chest giving his brother the side eye. "Do you hear yourself right now? Nigga, you didn't cheat on her with some random, you cheated on her with..."

"You don't know my wife. Our love is strong enough to overcome this shit. But, good thing she will never know because I'm cutting Nene's ass off and Egypt ass damn sure not going to let that secret out. Now, can we get off my love triangle."

"Yea, because the more you talk, the more I have to question your intelligence."

"Don't worry bro. As of tonight, I'm going to make it right with my wife. I will call Nene and let her know, this time we are completely done."

"Good luck with that shit. You know that girl not wrapped too tight. You better hope she goes away easily. You know what I don't understand is why your ass didn't leave that dingy bitch alone way back when. I mean once you knew who the fuck she was, you should have jetted with no hesitation."

"I did. When we ran into each other in Vegas that year, it was all about catching up. Then, we bumped into each other again and it's been on and off since."

"I wish your ass would have left that crazy bitch alone back in college," James shook his head disapprovingly.

"Yea, me too. Let me get out of here and get home." Aaron gave his brother another brotherly hug and packed up his things.

One his way home Nene called his phone nonstop. Giving in he finally answered her call. "What," he yelled into the phone.

"That's how we do? Why haven't you been answering my calls?"

Aaron took a deep breath knowing Nene was about to go all the way off on him. "Ne, I can't do this no more. I need to be all in with my wife and try to make this work. I allowed you to creep back into my life and... I'm sorry, but I can't do this. Serenity deserves better ard."

"Oh, so now you trying to play the perfect husband. You know what, do you. I'm not even mad at you. See you around Aaron." With that, Nene ended the call.

Aaron stared at his phone, surprised how well that went. He pulled up in his driveway and saw they had company. He was glad Serenity had somebody over, because this way she wouldn't be nagging him about leaving dinner. Plus, he needed a minute to himself. That conversation with Nene went a little too easy for his liking. When he walked into the house, he found Serenity and Shanita in the living room chatting.

"About time you got home. I left your plate on the table." Serenity told him.

"Thanks bae." As he was walking to the kitchen. He pulled out his phone to call James, but he noticed a message from Nene. His eyes grew big when he saw it was a picture of his house. He heard Serenity tell Shanita she was going upstairs to the bathroom. So, quickly he ran out the back door to the patio. He called Nene's phone and she picked up on the first ring.

"Yes sir."

"What the fuck are you doing?" He harshly whispered in the phone.

"Thinking about telling your wife about your dog ass. I mean, it's only right she knows the truth about you. No need for her to be walking around here like a fool right, since she deserves better?"

"Don't do this Nene. Look, I'm sorry ok. I just don't want to do this anymore. It was fun while it lasted, but I need to be a better man."

"Why now Aaron, huh?" Nene sobbed into the phone.

"Look, we can talk later ard."

"No, we're going to talk now nigga." Nene raised her voice.

Instead of responding, Aaron quickly ended his call when he heard Serenity come to the back door.

"What are you doing out here?"

"Oh, I thought I heard something. I was just checking it out. Them damn raccoons getting bad around here," Aaron quickly lied.

"Oh. Well, I'm about to kick my cousin out. Hurry up and eat and meet me upstairs." Serenity winked.

Aaron tucked his bottom lip getting aroused. It's been a minute since Serenity talked like that to him. "Word. I will be there in about ten. I'm about to smash this food, then I'm coming to smash something else."

Aaron watched as Serenity went back inside and took out his phone. He called Nene back, but she didn't answer. "Fuck," he cursed.

He didn't know if Nene was going to make good on her threat, but he hoped like hell she didn't. He really did want to make it work with Serenity and had known Nene wasn't going to make it easy for him to walk away. He had his reasons for wanting to make it work with Serenity. He didn't want to lose her to the next man. As selfish as it was, his ego couldn't allow it to happen. So, the best thing to do was get his shit together and do right.

Aaron stayed in the kitchen for a while trying to call Nene, but all his calls was going to voicemail. He finished his food and headed upstairs. By the time he got to his room Kian was in the bed with Serenity snuggled under her.

"What is this?" Aaron asked looking down at Kian.

"He's not feeling good. He's running a fever." Serenity told him.

"Are we still..." Aaron started to say.

Serenity looked up at Aaron giving him a stern look not believing he was even asking about sex. "No Aaron, our son sick," she hissed rolling her eyes.

"Right," Aaron snickered. "This is why I do what I do," he thought to himself. He grabbed his clothes and headed for the bathroom to take his cold shower. As he was stripping out his clothes, the thought of calling Nene again crossed his mind. But he fought temptation, knowing he couldn't go back. Even the thought of calling Egypt came to mind.

"Fuck, how I'm supposed to stay faithful when I can't get no pussy at home," he said out loud to himself.

Chapter 8

A month has gone by and Serenity saw a change in Aaron. He was home more and doing the things that he used to when they first met. She figured it had to be that little talk they had at Sunday dinner. So, all thoughts of him cheating went out the window.

Serenity's friendship with Markieff picked up right where they left off when they were teenagers. She loved that he was back and even happier that she was helping him spend time with Mykel. She was still baffled that a woman would keep their child away from their father over something so petty.

Now with Shanita coming around more, she and Serenity been spending a lot of time together as well. With everything that seemed to be going right in Serenity's life, she felt like her relationship with Egypt seemed to be growing apart. Serenity still didn't know what happened between Egypt and Shanita, but she wasn't about to beg Egypt to tell her either. Whatever it was couldn't have been that bad for Egypt to harbor feelings years later.

Walking out the bathroom, Serenity noticed Aaron had his suitcase on the bed.

"Morning bae," Aaron acknowledged her when she came into the room. He then walked over to his dresser to grab a few items he needed.

"Good morning," Serenity smiled, going over to the closet. She was about to say something to Aaron, but his phone rang. He just looked down at it and ignored it. "You're not going to answer that?" Serenity curiously asked.

"Nah, that's just James. I need to hurry up and pack." Aaron answered just as his phone went off again.

"Oh, well you want me to answer for you and tell him you're getting dressed?" She asked, walking towards the bed to grab it for him.

Aaron swiftly moved from the dresser and moved behind Serenity, wrapping his arms around her waist stopping her from answering the phone. "James will be alright. You go ahead and get ready for work. That nigga will see me in a little. Shit, he better be on his way to the airport." He said, kissing her neck.

"Oh, ok." Serenity gave Aaron the side eye. His phone went off again and usually if it was his brother calling this many times, he would have answered.

"I'm about to take a quick shower." Aaron then grabbed his phone and headed to the bathroom. Serenity watched him warily as he went into the bathroom closing the door. She stood there for a second trying to listen in on his call, but she couldn't hear with the shower on. It was just odd to her that he didn't want her to answer his phone and then took it in the bathroom with him. She hated to feel he was up to no good just when things between them was going so well.

"Ki, you dressed?" Serenity yelled down the hall.

"Yes, about to go downstairs to eat." Kian answered.

Serenity went back into her room and finished getting dressed herself. Once she was done, she hurried out the room and called Egypt. She didn't want to ask Aaron where he was going so asking Egypt was the next best thing, so she thought.

"Yea?" Egypt dryly answered.

"Ugh, why you answered the phone like that?"

"Like what Serenity?"

"Like I'm fucking bothering you."

"Look, I'm not in the mood for all that happy go lucky shit this morning. What's up, what are you calling me for?"

Serenity let out a snicker. She wanted to go off, but instead she asked what she needed from Egypt and kept it moving. She wasn't in the mood for her shit either. "Where is Aaron going?"

"Girl, what I tell you before. I am not his damn keeper." Egypt scoffed.

"Ugh, don't act like this," Serenity sighed.

"Act like what? Listen, your husband should be the one who tells your ass that information, not me. Look, I just sat down at my desk I will call you later." Egypt ended the call.

Serenity pulled the phone from her ear blankly staring at it. Aaron came into the kitchen getting her attention. "Hey, so I was thinking about having a nice little dinner Friday night, just me and you." Serenity blurted out.

"Aww, that sounds good bae, but this week is a conference. Then, I will have to go right to Dallas to check on the project we have out there. But I promise when I get back, I got you," Aaron said. He walked over and kissed her forehead. "Love you." Aaron felt like shit having to tell Serenity he wasn't going to be around for her birthday which was on that Friday. In his defense he had something special planned, so he played it off, knowing she was going to be pissed. He hurried and got his things together, kissed Serenity again and made his getaway.

Serenity stood in the middle of the kitchen and without her permission, hot tears started rolling down her face. They weren't tears of sadness, but of anger. She couldn't believe Aaron was back up to his old tricks using work as an excuse to cheat. Furthermore, she was pissed she has yet to find any proof of him having an affair. She was feeling stupid for not being able to prove what she knew. She thought if Aaron was cheating, he was doing a damn good job of hiding that shit.

"Ma, I'm ready," Kian told her, walking to the kitchen.

Serenity quickly wiped her face clean. "Ok baby, go ahead and start the car I'm coming."

"What's wrong?" Kian questioned seeing her face wet with tears.

"Nothing for you to worry about." Serenity forced a smile on her face.

"You sure? You know I'm here for you." Kian smiled, knowing it would make his mother laugh.

"I know baby. Thank you."

Serenity let out a sigh once Kian took off. She ran to the bathroom and cleaned her face. She touched up her makeup and hurried out the house. She wasn't able to make it to the school on time, so she had to walk Kian inside to sign him in. As she was going in, Markieff was coming out.

"Unk, what up," Kian said, giving him a high five."

"What's good Ki." Markieff looked over to Serenity and she was trying to avoid eye contact. He let out a snicker, knowing something was up. "Good morning Lucky. Your big head been missing in action last week. I miss my friend," Markieff pouted.

Serenity tucked a piece of her hair behind her ear and finally looked up. "I know, I...I been a little busy. How is everything going at the shop?"

"Everything is everything." Markieff paused and saw how red Serenity's eyes were and wanted to know why. "Yo, get that boy inside for school. I see we need to talk."

Serenity's brows raised. "How you come to that conclusion?"

"Your eyes always tell on your ass. Unless you been smoking, your eyes red for a reason." Markieff pointed.

Serenity hated how well Markieff knew her, but at the same time loved it. He was always that way with her and it was always hard to keep anything from him.

"Whatever. I will call you on my lunch break," she smirked.

"Bet." Markieff leaned over and kissed Serenity on the forehead. He then said his goodbyes to Kian and jogged off to his car.

Serenity got Kian signed into school and headed to work. As she was driving, she decided she wasn't in the mood to go in. She picked up her phone and called her supervisor, telling him she wasn't feeling well and wasn't coming in. Once that was handled, she headed back home.

****

On the other side of town, Aaron had to make a stop by the offices. When he walked in, Egypt was at her desk with a smug look plastered on her face.

"Good morning," Aaron spoke, ignoring the death stare Egypt was shooting his way.

"Whatever." Egypt responded.

Aaron stopped at her desk. "The hell wrong with you?"

"You, you're what's wrong with me." Egypt scoffed.

Aaron's head quickly whipped around making sure nobody was around to hear what Egypt said. He grabbed her arm, lifting her out her chair and dragged her into his office. He pushed her inside before slamming the door shut. He clenched his jaws as he stared her down.

"Care to explain what your problem is?" Aaron snarled.

"Why are you still married if you're still going to fuck around on my sister?"

Aaron sucked his teeth. "What are you talking about? I haven't cheated in months and frankly, I don't see where that is your business."

Crossing her arms over her chest, Egypt got up in his face. "Well, if you're not cheating, why you didn't tell her where you're going?"

"I did tell her."

"Then why she calling me asking questions. I'm a little disappointed in you. You hid so well for so long, but now you're slipping."

"What did you tell her when she called?"

"Nothing."

"Good. Although it's nothing to fucking tell, unless you going to out yourself."

"Yea, I can and I can tell her about Nene." Egypt smirked.

Aaron's eyes grew big. "How you know about that?"

"The last night we was together, I saw a text on your phone." Egypt paused and let out a snicker. "You know the funny part about it, I was mad at you like you was my nigga to start with. I was mad that you was cheating on me. So, one day after work I followed your ass. I saw y'all together. But how could I tell my sister the truth, without telling on myself."

Aaron was thankful for that. "Yea, well, I cut her ass off too. It's all about my wife now."

"It should have always been about your wife."

"Look who's talking. She's your sister." Aaron reminded her.

"And just why I should come clean. You know, I think I need to have one of those get right with Jesus moments and tell her everything."

"Why would you do something so stupid? No need to hurt her like that just to prove a fucking point to me. If you hate me that much, why the fuck you still working here? Huh, to keep looking in my face?"

"Nigga trust, it's all about the money honey. Where else am I going to find a gig that pays six figures to do nothing. Believe me, I'm over your ass."

Before Aaron could reply, James came walking in the office. He noticed the looks on both Aaron and Egypt's face only to wonder what he just walked into.

"Aaron, we need to get going bruh," James said, still looking between the two.

"I'm ready." Aaron replied, grabbing the paperwork he needed. "Ms. Beal, please email me that file I need." He said to Egypt as he walked out the office.

James waited until he and Aaron was alone in the car. He drove a few blocks before he opened his mouth to ask questions. "What was that back at your office? You two back fucking around?"

"Nah, nothing like that. I did find out why she stopped fucking with me. She knows about Nene." Aaron blurted out.

James couldn't help but let out a slight chuckle. "Let me guess, she threatened to tell?"

"Yea, she did. I told her what good would that do. I mean, she will have to tell on herself too. Why hurt Serenity because you hurt."

"This is why your ass shouldn't cheat. Hurt people hurt people. From the look on Egypt's face, you better do something to keep her mouth shut or be ready for Serenity to kill your ass."

Aaron didn't know what to do now. Just when he thought he was in the clear, here comes trouble. To his surprise, Nene stopped blowing up his phone and left well enough alone. Now, he had Egypt getting in her feelings yelling to tell something. Getting his attention was his buzzing phone. Looking down at, he saw it was Egypt's email. Attached was another message.

EgyptBeal@gmail.com: ***You know, a nice little raise would be nice. Oh, and a new car. I need an upgrade.***

Aaron laughed and turned his phone to James. "You see this shit?"

James was coming to a red light and turned to see what Aaron was crying about. He read the message and thought it was hilarious.

"This shit not funny man. I should have fired her ass a long time ago," Aaron scoffed.

"For what? That girl does her job. Just why you shouldn't have mixed business with pleasure."

"Yea, but I hired her ass off the strength of Serenity."

"Your ass paying for that shit now."

Aaron wasn't in the mood to continue the conversation. He picked up his phone and called Serenity. She didn't answer her cell, so he called her desk phone at work.

"Thanks for calling First National, Treasure speaking, how may I help you?"

Aaron's brows raised. "Yo, where is Serenity?"

"She called out sick." Treasure informed him.

"Ard, let me call her phone again," Aaron said and ended the call. He dialed Serenity's number but got the same results.

"You have reached Serenity Porter. I'm unavailable at the time." Aaron heard her voicemail pick up.

He waited until the greeting was over and left his message. "Hey bae. I called the job and see you called out. I was just calling to see how your day was going and to tell you I love you. I'm missing you already. Hit me back later."

James glanced over and peeped the puzzled looked that plastered Aaron's face.

"What's wrong?" James questioned.

"Nothing. Ren's sick and I was just checking on her. She seemed ok when I left, but she didn't even go to work."

"Umm, sounds like the rabbit got the gun." James joked.

"Fuck out of here. She's sick. Probably sleep or something." Aaron stated.

They pulled up to the airport. As they were walking to their gate, Aaron couldn't help but try calling Serenity again. Just like the other five times he called, she didn't answer.

.

Chapter 9

"Ugh, Markieff, give me my damn phone," Serenity whined.

"Hell no. You called out from work to chill with your boy because of your punk ass husband. So, why would I let you talk to him. Let his ass worry for a minute about where you at. I'm sure he called the bank looking for you."

"Yea, I'm sure he did." Serenity agreed. She gave up trying to fight him for her phone and plopped down in the chair. "What time you're going down to the barbershop?" She asked.

"I might roll by there around one or two. You coming with me?"

Serenity shrugged her shoulders. "I guess. I don't have nothing else to do." Serenity sat there with a blank look on her face and Markieff knew what that meant.

"Talk Lucky. What's going on in that big head?" Markieff hit her leg.

"What's wrong with me?" Serenity blurted out.

"What you mean?"

"Why is he cheating? Like, is something wrong with me?"

"Nah, we not doing this. Fuck that nigga ard. Look, nothing is wrong with you Lucky. Some men are stupid and don't appreciate what they have at home. But, if all your ass going to do is pout about this nigga and complain, take your ass home. If you're not going to do anything about it, why are you complaining?"

"What I'm supposed to do, leave him? I don't even know for sure if he's cheating."

"I told you, trust that gut feeling. If you really wanted to know the truth, you would have found it. One thing I know about females, y'all will get to the bottom of shit. If you're not ready to face the truth, don't go looking. Just remember, that shit you feeling right now will stay with you until you deal with this issue." Markieff lectured.

Drawing in a deep breath, Serenity slowly let it out. Everything Markieff was telling her was nothing but the truth. A part of her wanted to know and another part didn't. She wasn't sure if could handle the truth or even leave. Although she said she would, she didn't know if she could.

"Come on big head, let's go get something to eat," Markieff said, pulling her from her thoughts.

They left his house and went to one of their favorite hood spots for something to eat.

"I haven't been around here in years," Serenity said, looking out the window of the restaurant."

"Yea, I haven't been back here since we moved when I was younger. So many memories here Lucky." Markieff said as he started reminiscing about his younger days.

"It is," Serenity half smiled.

Taking a trip down memory lane herself, the good times flooded Serenity's mind. They stayed getting into something together. From her beating up girls for him to him keeping the boys away. Then, the one time they shared a special moment popped in her head, causing her lips to curl into a smile.

"What you're over there cheesing for?" Markieff inquired to know.

"Remember when we kissed over by old man Quell's store? You was trying to piss off Chrissy because she started talking to Antonio." Serenity laughed.

Markieff sucked his teeth. "Man, fuck her. She used me to get her ass some damn Jordan's. I knew she was jealous of you, so I had to make her ass mad."

"That's what you get. Should have been careful about which gold digger you laid down with, trying to be grown getting your little dick wet." Serenity teased.

"First off, I didn't lay down. I had her bent over with her ass in the air in the backseat of my Ford Explorer. Oh, ain't nothing little about my dick, so get your facts straight." Markieff laughed.

"Ugh, you so extra." Serenity shook her head.

"Yea, whatever you say. You over there thinking about the good days for real for real. You want to relive that memory?" Markieff leaned over with his lips puckered up for a kiss.

Serenity pushed him. "No, I don't want to relive that. Ugh, you always messing up a good moment."

"I'm just fucking with you. I don't want those chapped ass lips on mines."

Serenity stuck up her middle finger as she stood to her feet. "I'm going to bathroom."

Markieff nodded his head. He waved over the waitress and asked for the check. Serenity's phone started ringing again. He almost forgot he had it. Taking it out his pocket seeing it was Aaron again. A smirk covered his face as he hit the answer button.

"What's up A," Markieff answered.

"What the fuck you doing answering my wife's phone?" Aaron angrily hissed into the phone.

"Damn nigga, lighten the fuck up. The shit was ringing so I answered."

"Check this out. I pay that fucking bill so I would appreciate if you didn't answer my wife's phone. Now, put her on the line."

"I'm sorry, she's unavailable at the moment. I gave her a dose of something real good and she's knocked the fuck out. You know she wasn't feeling good, so I had to take care of my Lucky Charm. I will make sure she hit you up later. Enjoy your business trip bruh," Markieff said, ending the call. Serenity was coming, so he hurried and turned off her phone and placed it back in his pocket. He knew he was petty, but he wanted Aaron to feel how Serenity was feeling right now.

"What you do?" Serenity questioned, seeing the smirk plastered on Markieff's face.

"Pissed your husband off." Markieff honestly answered.

Serenity closed her eyes shaking her head from side to side. "You know what, I don't even want to know what you did. The way I'm feeling, I don't give a fuck at this point."

Markieff could hear the pain behind Serenity's words. He hated seeing her like this. So as her friend, he was going to get to the bottom of the mystery for her.

After hanging with Markieff, Serenity found her way home after picking up Kian from her parents. It was around six when she walked into her house and turned back on her phone. Kian told her Aaron called his phone a few times looking for her. Soon as her phone was powered on, it was going off. She let out a snicker and decided to answer it.

"Yea," she dryly answered.

"Serenity, I'm not in the mood to play with your ass. Why haven't you been answering your fucking phone and why is Markieff answering your shit?" Aaron snarled once he was on the line.

"Look, he had my phone when I went to the bathroom." Serenity halfway told the truth. "How was your day?"

"My day was fucked up, thanks to you. You know what, I don't even feel like talking to you right now. Goodnight." Aaron hissed, ending the call.

Taking her phone from her ear, she blankly stared at it. She let out a snicker and tossed her phone on the bed. Going to her closet she started her search. She was looking for anything that could answer all the questions she had.

"Ugh, something has to be in here," she sighed after looking through the pockets of Aaron's jeans.

"Ma, Shanita downstairs," Kian informed her.

"Tell her to come up here." Serenity wasn't about to stop what she was doing. She was determined to get the proof she needed.

"Hey girl." Shanita spoke, entering the room.

"Hey." Serenity dryly spoke.

Shanita sat down on the chair inside the room and watched Serenity for a second. When she saw her tossing clothes around, she looked at her warily. "Girl, what are you doing?"

"Come with me," Serenity said as she stormed out the room and went down to Aaron's office. "I'm trying to find something that can tell me if Aaron's cheating."

"Don't go looking for something if you're not ready to deal with the truth."

"At this point, I don't care. I am getting sick of wondering what he's doing every time he walks out this damn door...I just don't know."

"Ok, if you think he's cheating, why are you still married?"

"You sound just like him. What if I'm wrong. I would be leaving for nothing. This shit is fucking with me." Serenity reached up and started running her hands through her hair. She then swallowed the lump in her throat. Sliding down the wall, she sat down on the floor. "Girl, I feel so fucking dumb. If he is cheating, it will come to the light. But until then I have to sit back and wait, and that's the part that's fucking with me. I'm not happy in this marriage anymore because I don't know what he's up to."

"Like I said, leave his ass. No man is worth this stress."

"I know and deep down I still love him and want this to work. But he has to want this marriage to work." Serenity sighed. "Then, I have another problem."

Shanita raised her brows. "What?"

Serenity quickly got up from the floor and went to close the office door. She then turned around and smiled from ear to ear. "Ever since Markieff came back, I been thinking about the what ifs. If he never moved away, I wonder if we would have got together. Like, I know he likes to joke around and is a big flirt, but he's always been that way. Now, I just get this feeling he's not joking. I get butterflies when I'm around him. When we are together, I forget about everything. I wake up to good morning big head texts. I go to sleep to sweet dreams Lucky messages. Throughout the day, he asks me how my day is going. Aaron used to do those things. Now, all Aaron does is come home and fuss and start arguments over dumb shit. When he does that, it makes me think he's mad at the side bitch and comes home and takes it out on me. I know this sounds crazy, but I can't knock how I feel."

"Damn. I was coming over here to tell you to put me down with Markieff, but looks like you're still in love with his ass." Shanita smirked.

"What you mean still."

"Umm, don't play dumb. Girl, you know damn well you loved that boy back then. And don't you say he was like a brother to you, because I know it wasn't like that."

For a second Serenity forgot who she was talking to. Shanita may have been missing in action for a few years, but they all used to close. It was just that Egypt and Shanita grew closer because they were closer in age. Serenity's phone went off and it was Markieff telling her good night.

"Must be your boo." Shanita teased.

"No, it's Markieff."

"Like I said, your boo. Let me ask you, what's the reason you think Aaron's cheating?"

"He has done a whole three-sixty on me. I understand working long hours, but I just feel it in my gut that he's not most of the time. Even taking trips out of town. Every time I turn around, he's fucking working. Like this weekend, my damn birthday weekend he's gone. What else I'm supposed to think. At first, I understood because he was trying to move up at work. Once he got his promotion I thought he would be home more, but that shit didn't change. I guess I never complained before, so his ass continued to do him."

"I think you're thinking too much about it. It can be just that, work."

"Yea, well I hope so."

"What are you going to do about Markieff? Sounds like you have feelings for him and running."

Serenity let out a frustrated breath. "I don't know. I do know I love how he makes me feel when we're around each other."

"Deep," Shanita replied.

"Ok, enough about me. What the hell happened between you and Egypt?" Serenity asked, changing up the subject.

"I wish I knew myself." Shanita answered. But, in the back of her mind she had a feeling about what it was but wasn't sure. This was also why she stayed away for so long.

Serenity's doorbell went off, causing her to get up. She checked her peephole before opening the door and saw it was Treasure and her son Justice.

"Hey girl. I came to check on your ass since you wasn't answering your phone. Oh, and Aaron called my phone twice, asking if we was together. So, I had to drop by." Treasure informed her walking into the house.

"Kian home?" Justice asked.

"Yea, he's in his room." Serenity told him, giving him a hug.

Treasure walked over to the couch and sat down.

"T, you remember my cousin Shanita?" Serenity asked.

"Yea, hey girl." Treasure spoke. "Now, where your ass been all day?" She added, getting all in Serenity's business.

"Out with her boo?" Shanita blurted out before Serenity could answer.

Serenity playfully sucked her teeth. "Ugh, can I tell my own business?" She playfully rolled her eyes then answered the question. "I was with Markieff."

"Umm. And what was y'all doing that had you not answering your phone all damn day." Treasure teased.

"What we always do when we are together, talk and chill."

"And that's why Aaron's ass in his feelings?" Treasure's brows raised.

"Girl, Markieff answered my phone and said something to Aaron. What he said, I don't even know and really don't care. Aaron on some other shit and I don't know what to do anymore. I tossed our closet upside down trying to find something, but I got nothing"

Treasure put up her hands. "Hold up, I thought y'all was good?"

"Yea, I thought so too. This morning he was acting real shady about his damn phone. Any other time when James calls him, he will tell me to get it and tell him he's getting dressed or whatever. This morning he didn't want me to touch the phone."

"Oh yea, that nigga up to something. Have you checked his office?" Knowing his ass, that's where all the evidence could be." Treasure pointed out.

Serenity gave it some thought and it made sense. She couldn't find anything at home and never thought about his work office. With Aaron being gone, she had the perfect way to get in there to do her snooping.

"T, we can go to his office tomorrow. I will get Egypt to let us in." Serenity nodded her head up and down, feeling like she just might come up with something to put her mind at ease.

"Ren, you sure you want to do this? Remember, don't go looking for something when it could be absolutely nothing. I mean, other than working a lot you have nothing that results in him cheating. I just think since the thought is in your head, every little thing he does will have you paranoid that he's doing something." Shanita preached.

"Fuck that, my girl is not paranoid about shit. That nigga cheating." Treasure said.

Shanita looked over to Treasure and rolled her eyes. It was something about her that didn't sit too well with her. And the fact that she was loud and ghetto didn't help. "Ren, all I will say is try talking to him and see if he will tell you the truth. Going behind his back snooping is asking for trouble. Hell, if no bitch came forward that nigga not cheating. You know these side bitches be extra now a days and be doing the most. I just don't want you going looking and it's nothing there and start trouble." Shanita give Treasure a smug look before rolling her eyes again.

Serenity was taking in what both ladies was saying, but her mind was already made up. She was going to search that office and get to the bottom of this bullshit.

"Can I ask you something?" Shanita asked.

"Sure." Serenity replied.

"If you find out he's cheating, what are you going to do? Are you going to leave him and let the next bitch win and take what's yours?"

"Hell yea she is, shit. Why stay with a nigga that's not obeying his vows?" Treasure yelled out.

"Because in those vows it says for better or worse. Not every marriage is perfect." Shanita shot back.

"See, that's bullshit. If a man steps out on his wife, why should the wife stay? Aaron has no reason to cheat."

"How do you know that?" Shanita smirked.

Treasure let out a chuckle. "You know what, let me go. Renny, see you tomorrow at work. Justice, let's go," Treasure yelled. She stood to her feet and started walking for the door.

Serenity walked her out to her car and gave her a hug.

"Sorry about my cousin but she just looking out, just like you. Thank you for coming to check on me." Serenity smiled.

"Anything for my girl." Treasure leaned over and gave Serenity a hug.

"Call me when you get home. Bye Justice." Serenity waved. She then stepped back as Treasure backed out the driveway.

Shanita came out the house and headed over to Serenity. "Girl, I need to get out of here. My man on his way over to my crib."

"Alright now, somebody about to get them some." Serenity teased.

"I hope. Dude been on some other shit lately. Hell, I'm starting to think it's another woman in the picture."

"See, now I think you're being funny. But it's cool, fuck Aaron and that hoe."

Shanita hands quickly flew to her mouth. "I didn't mean it like that. Sorry if that was insensitive."

"Girl, you're good. I'm over it all." Serenity waved her hands.

"Ok. Call me tomorrow if you want to go out for drinks or something."

"I will."

Serenity went upstairs and got herself ready for bed. After her shower, she checked on Kian. He was fast asleep to her surprise. Usually, she would have to fuss for him to get off his Xbox. She went back to her room and got in her bed. She reached for her phone and checked for her messages or missed calls. The only message she had was the one Markieff's been sending her. She thought about calling Aaron but pushed that thought out her mind just as fast as it came. He went off on her for no reason, so it was fuck him at this moment. She loved Aaron but hated feeling uncertain in her marriage. Closing her eyes she drifted off to sleep.

Moments later, Serenity heard a noise. Her eyes popped open and she heard it again. She swung her covers off her and sat in the bed.

"Who the fuck is at my door this time of the night," Serenity growled. She slipped her feet into her slippers and grabbed her robe and headed for the door. The soft knocks intensified to hard banging and she knew who was on the other end.

"Lucky, come open the door." Markieff yelled.

Serenity opened the door and found Markieff swaying back and forth. She could smell the liquor on his breath. His eyes were bloodshot red and Serenity knew he was highly intoxicated.

"You didn't text me back Lucky. I just wanted to make sure you was good. Why you didn't text back?" Markieff slurred.

"Boy, how did you even make it over here in your condition? Why did you leave home like this?"

"Because you didn't text back. You always text back Lucky. I...I was worried."

Serenity shook her head and pulled Markieff inside. "Lay your ass down on the couch. You're not going home like this. I will go grab you a blanket."

"Yes ma'am." Markieff smirked. But instead of following directions, he followed her upstairs.

"Didn't I tell you to stay downstairs?" Serenity laughed.

"You did, but what I wanted was up here." Markieff walked up behind Serenity while she was inside the closet. He gripped her by her hips and pulled her closer to him and kissed her neck.

Serenity jumped and turned around with her eyes wide open. "Kieff, what the hell are you doing?"

"Something I should have done a long time ago. I wanted you from the first time I laid eyes on you but didn't know how to tell you. You are the one that got away and I'm sorry, but Aaron don't deserve you anymore." Markieff confessed his love as he backed Serenity into the wall. Without giving it a second thought, he placed his hands on each side of her face and kissed her passionately. When he saw Serenity wasn't resisting, he lifted her up.

"Markieff, wait, we can't do this. This is wrong." Serenity stated.

"Yea, but it feels so fucking right." Markieff placed Serenity back down on her feet, but he got down on his knees. As he untied her robe he glared into her eyes, looking for any signs for him to stop. He placed his hands on her waist and slowly moved them down as he took her pants off. He licked his lips seeing Serenity wasn't fighting to stop him. Leaning forward he kissed her lips as his hand made it's way inside her panties.

"Damn that pussy soaking wet." He moaned against her lips.

"This is wrong." Serenity reminded him.

"I know, but I don't give a fuck and neither should you."

"I'm married."

"Yea, well that title don't mean shit without a bond. You don't love that nigga like you love me." A smirk covered Markieff's face while he dropped down to his knees. Using the wall for support he lifted Serenity up again, as her legs hung over his shoulders.

"If you don't put me down," Serenity wiggled.

"Yo, chill and shut up." Markieff grinned.

He started rubbing her D sized breasts, massaging her hardened nipples. Serenity kept mumbling how wrong this was, but all her cries fell on deaf ears.

Markieff didn't give a fuck at this point and was going for what he wanted. Seductively a smirk covered Markieff's face. Using two fingers, he stuck them inside of Serenity's soaked pussy.

"Taste it," Serenity moaned.

"Oh, I had plans to."

With that being said, Markieff licked his way around the folds of her pussy lips until he came in contact with the tip of her clit. He then sucked hard on her clit, causing her scream out.

"Fuck Markieff, this shit feels so good," she moaned, not caring about her marriage anymore. She closed her eyes feeling the ecstasy building up already. Thinking to herself, she could have sworn Markieff took a class on how to eat pussy.

Slowly Markieff dipped his fingers in and out while his warm tongue played with her love button. Gripping the back of his head, Serenity tightened her grip feeling herself about to explode.

"Umm, you're about to make me cum." Serenity announced.

"Then do it. Let that shit out Lucky," Markieff encouraged her.

"I'm cumming, oh yes, I'm cumming." Just as Serenity was about to explode, her alarm went off and immediately she came back to reality.

Her chest was heaving up and down feeling the effect of her dream. She looked down and saw her hands was inside her pants and the cum on her thighs felt like glue.

"What the fuck just happened?" She thought to herself. "Damn, that dream felt so real."

Right on cue, like any other morning Serenity's phone beeped alerting her she had a message. She knew it was Markieff telling her good morning. She reached over and grabbed her phone. She glanced down at it staring for a second. Her dream had her wondering what was going on with her. It was like Markieff pops back up and her mind and body started having a mind of its own. Without responding she placed her phone down and started getting ready for work.

"Ma, are you and daddy getting a divorce?" Kian blurted out as they sat the table eating breakfast.

Serenity damn near choked on her coffee. She was caught off guard from what Kian just said. "Ki, why would you ask me something like that?"

"Umm. Will I get in trouble if I tell you something?"

Serenity's brows raised as a puzzled look covered her face. "Something like what?"

"Well, I heard you talking last night, and I know you think daddy is cheating."

Serenity knew she shouldn't have been talking openly with the girls knowing Kian was still up. She walked over and sat next to Kian.

"Baby, you don't worry about that ok. Me and your father are ok." Serenity said, trying to clear up what Kian may have heard last night. She didn't know what else to say, but she knew she had to say something.

"But, it's true. Daddy thinks I'm stupid because he didn't want me to tell."

Now Serenity was curious as to what Kian had to say. "Tell what?"

"Am I going to get in trouble?"

"No baby."

"After my football game, daddy gave me his phone while him and Uncle Markieff was talking. I was playing a game on the phone and…and some lady sent a picture. She didn't have no clothes on. Daddy got mad at me for looking, but I was just trying to play a game. He told me not to tell you about it."

Serenity's eyes got big. She couldn't believe her ears. Hearing what Kian said definitely confirmed what she already knew. She plastered a fake smile on her face. "I'm sure the lady had the wrong number baby. Your daddy is not stupid to let something like that happen." Serenity said, trying to pacify Kian from the truth. She couldn't believe her son knew about her husband's cheating ways and had the proof she needed.

"Ki, keep this little talk between me and you ok?"

"I got you mommy. So, does this mean y'all getting a divorce? Because if so, I want to stay with you." Kian pointed out.

Serenity couldn't help but laugh at Kian. "Boy come on before you be late for school."

"Ma, does this make me a snitch since I told on daddy?" Kian questioned.

"No baby, you're not a snitch."

On the drive to Kian's school, Aaron was calling Serenity's phone. She didn't bother to answer it. She had so much on her mind and hearing Aaron's voice would have just pushed her overboard, so it was best to ignore him until she could think straight. When she got to work, she sat in a daze most of the morning. It was now lunch time and Serenity walked into the break room. Treasure was already seated at the table waiting for her to come in. When Serenity sat down the tears she had been fighting back all day came pouring down her face. Treasure didn't know what was going on because Serenity still haven't told her what Kian said.

"No ma'am, not here," Treasure said, getting up to get some tissue. She walked over to Serenity and wiped her face. "What is going on with you?"

"You ever just woke up and been on some different shit? Like, you didn't give a fuck about anything and wanted to do you, even if it meant hurting somebody else's feelings?"

Treasure tilted her head, not liking the sound of Serenity's voice. "Ren, what happened?"

Before Serenity could answer, a few other workers came waltzing into the break room. Toni was amongst the group. She noticed the discomfort on Serenity's face and thought about adding to her misery.

"Aww, did your fine ass husband finally wake up and see he could do better?" Toni taunted.

Serenity's sorrow was quickly replaced with anger. Toni picked the wrong day to want to start shit with her. At this point, Serenity didn't give a damn about that job. She got out her seat and charged towards Toni. Before Toni could register what was going on, Serenity's fist was coming full force to her face.

"Bitch, I told you I wasn't the one to play with," Serenity screamed as she drilled her fist forcefully into Toni's face. "You keep running that big ass mouth of yours."

"Bitch, get off me." Toni cried, swinging her arms wildly trying to connect with Serenity's face.

Treasure stood there with her arms crossed over her chest. The girl that came in with Toni thought about breaking it up, but the way Serenity went breast mode on Toni, she left well enough alone. Moment's later, the door came open and Lamont rushed in.

"Yo, why y'all just standing there?" He questioned.

"Shit, that girl needs her ass beat and Serenity needs to relieve some stress." Treasure shrugged her shoulders.

Lamont stood there for a second and watched as Serenity tossed Toni around like it was nothing. He had to let out a chuckle and say, "Shit Toni. With all that fucking mouth, I thought your ass had hands. Serenity working your ass." Just as he was about to take out his phone, the door opened again and he rushed over, acting like he was breaking up the fight.

The other girl did the same, but Treasure just stood there. Toni deserved everything she was getting for talking so much trash and starting with Serenity. Lamont was able to pull Serenity off Toni and lift her up, carrying her out the room.

"Put me down. I'm not done with that bitch. You're joking about my husband and shit, you're probably the one fucking his ass. You dirty bitch. Put me down," Serenity continued to yell.

"Yo, chill out girl." Lamont told her. He carried her all the way out the back door. He finally put her down and looked her up and down. She didn't have no signs of just being in a fight. "Damn, did she even pinch your ass?"

Serenity let out a snicker as she bent over breathing heavy. "No, she didn't. Her ass doesn't have no fight in her. She got that ass beat North Philly style."

"I see that. But what's up? Why you in here fighting, risking your job?"

"Fuck her and this job. Bitch picked the wrong day to fuck with me."

The back door opened and out came the police. "Mrs. Porter?" One of the officers asked.

"Yea, that's me." Serenity answered.

The officer took out his cuffs and started walking towards Serenity. "Ma'am I'm sorry, but your under arrest."

"For what?" Serenity asked in disbelief.

"Assault. Ms. Hill is pressing charges." The officer informed her.

"Great." Serenity didn't even argue with the officer. She turned around, allowing him to place the cuffs on. As she was being escorted through the bank, she gave Toni a death stare before turning to Treasure. "Call Egypt and tell her to come get me please."

"I got you," Treasure ensured her.

Serenity was placed in the backseat of the police car and couldn't believe how her day was starting. But at least she found out some valuable information. The ride to the station she thought about all the signs she possibly missed with Aaron and his cheating, and was mad at herself for not noticing it sooner. Now that she knew, she still wanted to know why Aaron would mess up their marriage like that.

Chapter 10

Aaron sat at a table full of his business partners blankly staring off in space. He could hear the president of the company talking, but nothing he was saying was catching Aaron's attention. His mind been clouded ever since Markieff answered Serenity's phone the day before. It didn't help that she didn't call or text this morning. Here it was going on noon and he haven't heard from her. Aaron's boss was now calling his name, but he was too far gone in his thoughts, he didn't hear him.

"Aaron," James nudged him, getting his attention.

"Yea." Aaron jumped out his seat, snapping out his fog. He looked around hearing everyone around him snickering.

"Aaron, are you ok?" Mr. Peterson asked. "You seem a little distracted today."

"Yea, Yea, I'm good." Aaron said, fixing his tie.

"Ok, tell us about the projects you have coming up. Where are you with the deal with Boeing?"

Aaron grabbed his paper and started reading his notes to the group. Once Aaron was finished, his boss had a few questions for him.

"Have you talked anymore with your father in law about his properties? He has a lot of real estate that could bring the company some serious cash flow."

"We talked, but he's not trying to sell." Aaron informed him.

"Come on A, you have to get this man to sell at least of those properties. Look, you pull that off you will have that corner office. After that, you will be looking to make partner."

Aaron let out a frustrated breath of air. It was rumored that the only reason he got his promotion is because Mr. Peterson found out that Benny was his father in law. Mr. Peterson had his reasons for wanting Benny's properties, but Aaron didn't know what those reasons was. After the meeting was over Aaron went down to the hotel bar. He ordered his drink and pulled out his phone. He was shocked to see no type of missed call or text from Serenity.

"You good bruh?" James asked, taking a seat next to Aaron.

"Yea, I'm good."

"Don't look like it." Carl, one of their coworkers pointed out.

The bartender came back with Aaron's drink. He grabbed his beer and guzzled it down. It only took him seconds to finish it. He then slammed the empty bottle down and signaled for the bartender to bring him another one.

"Damn the way you tossed that Heineken back, seem like woman problems?" Carl joked, not knowing his statement had some truth behind it.

"Fuck you Carl," Aaron scoffed. This time, he took a few sips of his beer and let out a sigh. "Do Serenity seem like the cheating type," he blurted out.

"Oh, shit. That rabbit got the gun cocked and loaded. That bitch karma coming around I see," James laughed.

"Haha, laugh at my pain." Aaron said flatly. "I'm being serious."

"Why? Because her male best friend answered her phone?" James pointed out.

"Damn, who side you on?" Aaron sucked his teeth.

"The right side. Shit, I hope she is cheating on your nut ass. I been telling you to get right and leave Nene loco ass alone. She the type of chick that don't go away easy. Now you're sitting here feeling like Serenity's been feeling when you don't answer all her calls and shit. Only difference between y'all, she has every right to feel how she feel, you don't. That's your guilt catching up with your ass. That damn girl not cheating on you."

Lifting his beer Aaron took another sip. Maybe he was overthinking things. He knew Markieff didn't like him and the feeling was mutual. Aaron then remember he snapped on her when she finally answered her phone the night before. He figured she might have been mad and wasn't calling him. Taking out his phone, he called her. The phone went straight to voicemail, making him leave a message.

"Hey bae. Didn't hear from you all day and I know why. I'm sorry about snapping last night. Had a rough day and was taking my anger out on the wrong person. I was just checking on you. Hit me back once you get this message. Love you."

"Let me ask you something. What would you do if Serenity is cheating? You wouldn't think she had every right to?" James quizzed Aaron, curious of what his answer would be.

Aaron shrugged his shoulders. "I don't know. I never thought about her stepping out on me. Shit, ok, if she is cheating, we fucking even. But I will beat the shit out of dude."

Carl shook his head and decided to share his story with Aaron. "See, that ego. I never understood why dudes cheat, but soon as females flip that shit and cheat, we get mad. I learned the hard way, don't dish out what you can't handle. It took for me to get hurt see that men hurt too. When I found out that Sandra was playing me that shit broke me down. I was just like you, thinking my girl wasn't going to leave. I just knew I could apologize and all would be forgiven. When I saw her with that bull Manny from South Philly, I was ready to kill that nigga. Shit opened my eyes."

"Damn nigga, I didn't know Sandra cheated on you." James commented.

"Yea, not something I want to broadcast to the world. Look, I never said anything because shit made me seem like a sucka." Carl replied

"Shit like that is just why I try telling Aaron hard-headed ass to cut it out with that chick. Serenity is a good girl bruh. Chill before you lose her for good, for a bitch that's probably only doing this to piss your wife off." Aaron expressed sincerely.

"I hear you man. I told you, I did cut off Nene. I purposely told Serenity I wasn't going to be in town for her birthday. So, when I go home Friday, I will make it up to her. I will cook that dinner she wanted and make love to her like I never have before. Shit, we haven't had sex in months. Time for me to show my baby some attention." Aaron said.

"Tell me this. Are you getting your shit together because you feel threatened by Markieff, or you really want to be with your wife? If not, you need to end shit now. Get a divorce and let that cheating shit go before shit go left and somebody get hurt. Trust me, shit can get crazy.

"I got his." Aaron answered, avoiding responding to James' statement about Markieff.

"Ard, enough of that shit. Time to talk business. You need to call Benny and get on top of this shit before you lose your job." James insisted.

Aaron picked up his phone and right away he called Benny.

"Aaron, what's going on?" Benny beamed on the other end of the phone.

"Mr. Benny, I know we talked about this before, but my boss really thinks we can help you expand your business. Maybe when I get home we can talk a little more and I can show you some numbers."

"Damn Aaron, Serenity didn't tell you, I don't own my properties anymore. I stepped down from all of them."

"What! I mean oh wow, what happened? She didn't tell me anything. When did this happen? " Aaron asked.

"I gave over my businesses to Markieff. You should call him and set something up. It's a good thing he and Serenity are close." Been gloated.

Aaron's jaws clenched. He was pissed that Benny didn't call him before he stepped down from his companies. Furthermore, he was mad Serenity didn't mention none of this to him.

"Aaron, you still there?" Benny checked once the line got silent.

"Yea, yea, I'm here. I guess I need to call Markieff and see if he wants to sit down and talk numbers." Aaron replied.

"Yea, you do that. Now, I have to go. Me and the wife headed to Paris."

Before Aaron could say anything, Benny ended the call.

"Fuck," Aaron cursed out loud.

"What's wrong?" James questioned.

"Benny stepped down and gave everything to Markieff. Like what the fuck is up with this damn dude. Benny's ass knew what time it was, and knew we was interested in his properties. All he had to do was give them to me and boom, the company could have taken over. Now I have to go through this nigga Markieff for the shit. Ugh, I don't even know why Mr. Peterson wants anything to do with it. I mean, it's two barbershops, a hotel and a few restaurants."

"Stop downplaying this shit. Mr. Benny has an exclusive clientele list." James pointed out.

"Whatever. Look, I'm going back to my room to chill." Aaron paid his bar tab and headed to his room. On his way up he tried calling Serenity's phone again. He let out a frustrated breath of air, hearing her voicemail play. "Ok, you're being stupid right now. It's almost 4:00pm and I haven't heard from you yet. Call me, now."

When Aaron got to his room, he went straight to his bag and took out his other phone. Of course, he had a few missed calls from Nene. He chuckled to himself and tossed the phone back in his bag. He didn't even know why he still had his spare phone being that he cut her off. Stripping out his clothes, he took a quick shower. When he got out, there was a knock at his door.

"Jay, I said I wanted some time to myself." Aaron hissed, opening the door.

"Yea, I know, but check. Your girl calling my damn phone, but she called and said Serenity got arrested."

"Arrested, for what?"

"What you think? I told you the shit you got going on is a little too close to home, but you got a hard fucking head talking about y'all got this shit under control."

"Damn, ard man look, I gotta bounce." Aaron said, going over to his bag.

"Dude you know damn well you can't go until Thursday. We got too much on the line. I'm sure Serenity will be good. Just call her ass. But you can't go home yet."

Aaron flopped down on the bed and buried his face in his hands. "Fuck," he yelled. "This shit is getting too real for me. I gotta fix it."

"You think," James snickered.

Getting his phone, Aaron called Serenity again and her voicemail picked up. He left another message, letting her know he knew what happened. He felt bad for snapping on her for not answering her phone.

"Come Friday, baby girl won't be mad at me," Aaron smiled, thinking he had all the answers.

"Sounds good. Because it seems like you need to be on her good side in order to close this damn deal with Markieff." James reminded him.

"Nigga please, I'm not kissing that nigga ass for shit."

"Yo, put your fucking pride and ego to the side. At the end of the day, we still have a fucking job to do. And closing deals is one of them. You know what, fuck it. I'm done talking to your hard-headed ass. Just remember, you reap what you sow, positively and negatively." James preached and left Aaron alone with his thoughts.

Aaron stuck up his middle finger as the door shut behind James. He knew everything he was saying was true, but he hated he had to go to Markieff for anything.

Chapter 11

"Girl, I'm so happy you finally whooped that bitch ass. Toni been begging for that shit far too fucking long," Treasure cheered, getting in the car. She just picked Serenity up from jail.

"Exactly. Thank God for that officer. He was nice and didn't even charge me. He said he knows Toni's ass and thought she deserved what she got too. You got my phone?"

"Yea, it's in your bag in the back. Your husband been calling."

"Fuck him." Serenity turned around and reached in the backseat for her bag. Taking her phone out, she played her messages from Aaron. She snickered hearing him apologizing for his first message.

"You want to go to Applebee's'? They have drinks for a dollar."

"Sure. I need a drink or two."

They got to Applebee's and didn't waste any time taking advantage of the drink special.

"Ok now, I left your ass alone all damn day, but after seeing you snap on Toni's bitch ass, something is going on. Now that you have some drinks in your system, start talking." Treasure demanded.

Serenity sucked in some air and closed her eyes. "Aaron is cheating."

"Damn, I had high hopes for his ass. How did you find out?"

"Girl, Kian. He overheard us talking last night, and this morning he told me he saw a picture of this chick on Aaron's phone."

"Oh hell nah, see that nigga need his ass beat for that shit. Have you talked to Aaron about this shit yet?"

"No, I haven't. I been avoiding his calls."

"Did Kian tell you what the girl look like?"

Serenity shook her head. "Nah, he only saw her nasty ass body."

"What are you going to do about this shit?"

Serenity shrugged her shoulders up and down. "I don't even know. I have a week to think while his ass away on this business trip."

"Humph, you sure it's a business trip?"

"Right," Serenity agreed and let out a snicker. "Ugh, this shit just came out of nowhere."

"No boo-boo, this shit ain't come from nowhere. Like you said, those signs been there but you haven't been paying attention. Example. Late nights at work, extra business, his mood swings when you haven't even done shit. You just didn't want to believe it. Ren, what made you even think he was cheating?"

Serenity thought about the question. She wasn't even sure when she picked up on Aaron's change of behavior. Then, it hit her. It was about a year ago. He came home in a bad mood because of something that happened at work. Thinking back, she was now sure he was probably mad at his side chick. From that day, it seemed like when he was pissed him off, he came home taking it out on her.

"Why didn't he just leave," Serenity blurted out.

"You know how these dudes do. They want the best of both worlds."

Moments later, Shanita came over to the table. "Sorry I'm late. I had to pick up my homegirl. She had a bad day at work. She got into a fight with one of her..." Before Shanita could finish her sentence, Toni was approaching the table.

"Lawd, please tell me this bitch is not your homegirl?" Treasure scowled, looking towards Shanita.

"What the fuck Shanita, you said we was coming out with your cousin." Toni spoke.

"This is my cousin." Shanita answered.

Toni snickered. "Hold up, you never said Serenity was your cousin. You mean to tell me you..."

Serenity stood up, causing Toni to shut up and step back.

"Ren, you got lucky not getting charged earlier. Don't even let that hoe take you there right now." Treasure said, grabbing Serenity's arm.

"I'm cool T. I'm not even going to touch this hoe. I'm ready to go. Shanita, you need some new friends." Serenity stated, walking away.

Toni waited until Serenity and Treasure was out the door before she said anything. "Why didn't you tell me that was your damn cousin?"

"I didn't see the need to tell you, that's why." Shanita shot back.

Toni shook her head. "I can't believe this shit... You know what, never mind. You foul as hell. You said you knew Serenity, you never mentioned the bitch was your cousin."

"What does it matter." Shanita shrugged her shoulders.

"You know why it matter..." Toni started to yell, but the manager came over.

"Ma, either you keep it down or I'm going to ask you to leave." The manager pointed out.

"Don't worry, I'm gone." Toni informed her, marching out the door.

***

Serenity and Treasure rode in silence as they headed back to the bank to get Serenity's car. Treasure could tell Serenity was lost in her thoughts and didn't want to bother her. She could image the pain she was feeling. Treasure had her share of heartbreaks, but she knew the type of pain Serenity was feeling was worse. Pulling up to the bank, Treasure broke her silence.

"You're going to be ok?"

Serenity nodded her head up and down. "Yea, I'm good. I think I will take a few days off and get my mind right. I will let Kian stay with my parents. With Aaron being gone, I can use this time to think about how I will approach this situation with him. I'm sure Kian wasn't making up what he saw on that phone."

"Alright boo. Call me if you need me. I will come check on you tomorrow."

"No, you don't have to. I will call you when I'm ready for company." Serenity retorted.

"Oh ok."

"My bad girl, I didn't mean to come off like that," Serenity quickly apologized.

"Hey, no need for that. I understand. Just call me when you're ready to talk."

Serenity reached over and gave Treasure a hug before getting out the car. Treasure waited until Serenity was safely inside her car before she pulled off. Getting in her car, Serenity sat there for a few seconds. She then called Egypt and pulled off.

"Yes Serenity?" Egypt answered the phone.

Not even saying anything, Serenity hung up. She was getting sick of Egypt's attitude. Soon as she got her situation under control with Aaron, she was going to get to the bottom of Egypt and Shanita's problem. She was enjoying having Shanita around again, but missed her big sister. Serenity's phone went off causing her to slightly chuckle seeing it was Egypt calling back.

"Yep," Serenity dryly answered.

"How you're going to call my phone and don't even say anything then hang up? That was rude." Egypt fussed into the phone.

"Because you answered like somebody fucking bothering you. I don't have time for your snobby ass attitude over something that you won't even tell me about."

"Whatever Serenity. What was you calling for?"

"I was going to tell you what I found out about Aaron. I'm not even in the mood anymore. I will call you tomorrow." Serenity said, ending the call. She then called Kian, to see how his day went and to tell him good night. When she got home, she started herself a nice warm bath. Turning on some music she got comfortable in her tub allowing the water to relax her body. She closed her eyes and almost jumped out from the thoughts that crossed her mind.

"Ugh, why am I dreaming about him like this," she asked herself out loud. She looked around as if somebody else was in the room reading her mind. She closed her eyes again and her lips curled into a smile, getting lost in her thoughts. She felt guilty for dreaming about another man, but she couldn't stop them from flooding her mind.

The next day, Serenity woke up on a mission. She pulled out her laptop and logged into her At&t cellphone account scrolling the bill. She was looking for any number that Aaron seem to call the most.

Nothing seemed to stick out to her. Then, she thought about his business phone.

"Oh, that sneaky mutherfucker," she mumbled to herself.

Laying her laptop down, she got up from the bed and went over to her closet. Before she could get something out to wear, her phone was dancing across the nightstand. It was Treasure calling. Serenity wasn't in the mood to talk so she didn't answer. Treasure called back, but hung up. The phone then beeped, alerting Serenity that she had a text. Thinking this might be important, she grabbed her phone and called Treasure back. Soon as Treasure got on the line, she started yapping away.

"Girl, how about Toni just left out of Mr. Joe's office. All I heard was Toni yelling he better do something, or she was cutting him off. I think that bitch fucking his ass." Treasure informed her.

Serenity opened her mouth to reply, but her line beeped, letting her know she had another call. After hearing what Treasure said, Serenity let out a snicker seeing the bank's main number flashing across her screen.

"T, somebody from the bank calling. I will text you," Serenity said and quickly clicked over. "Hello," she dryly answered, knowing this call was about to be on some bullshit.

"Mrs. Porter, how are you doing this morning?" Mr. Joe asked, coming on the line.

"I'm fine."

"Good. I was hoping to see you at work today, because I needed to talk to you. I hate doing this over the phone, but since I know you took off for the rest of the week, it's just best I informed you now."

"Inform me of what?" Serenity scoffed.

"Because of your behavior yesterday, we decided to let you go. I'm sorry, but we can't afford for you to make the workplace a hostile environment."

"This some bullshit. What about Toni? She instigated that shit and got what she fucking deserved."

"It doesn't matter what Nene...I mean Toni did. You can't go attacking people."

Serenity let out a snicker. "Nene huh. This shit sounds personal now. You know what, fuck you and that job and that bitch you fucking. I hope your ass catch something you can't get rid of fucking that bitch." With that, Serenity ended her call. Out of anger, she threw her phone against the wall. When she saw it shatter into pieces, she regretted throwing it.

"Fuck," she cursed going over to pick it up. The thought of running to At&t to get another phone crossed her mind. Instead, she decided to wait. This way, she didn't have to hear her phone ringing and seeing Aaron's name across her screen. Getting back in the bed, she grabbed her remote and clicked on the television. She had to catch up on a few shows and that's what she was going to dedicate her day doing.

Serenity fell asleep at some point of the day and was awakened by the banging at her front door. At first she was going to ignore it, until she heard Egypt yelling for her to come open the door because their parents been trying to reach her. She slowly moved out the bed then the thought of something being wrong with Kian put some fire under her feet. She ran downstairs and swung the door opened.

"Is my baby ok?" Serenity panicked .

"His bad ass is just fine. Mommy said she been calling you since this morning. She called your job and they said they fired your ass. Oh, your punk ass husband been calling too."

Serenity sucked her teeth at the mention of Aaron's name.

"You still on this bullshit about him cheating. Girl, if you don't..."

"The bitch sent a picture to his phone." Serenity blurted out, cutting her off. "Kian saw the picture and told me about." Serenity flopped down on the couch and covered her face with her hands.

Egypt's mouth formed the letter O, caught off guard from Serenity's confession. She eased down in the loveseat across from Serenity. She swallowed hard, trying to rid the lump in her throat.

"What...what did Aaron say about it?" Egypt nervously asked.

"Nothing because I haven't mentioned it to him. I don't even know what to say."

Egypt closed her eyes and tears came rolling down her face. She knew it was only a matter of time before Serenity found out the truth. She didn't know how she could come clean about Aaron's affair with Nene, when she had one with him herself. She hated she put herself in this situation, because the hurt painted on Serenity's face pulled at her heart strings. When she was sleeping with Aaron, Serenity's feelings never crossed her mind.

"Ren, you in there?" They heard Treasure yelling on the other side of the door as she knocked on it.

"Come in T," Serenity yelled.

Treasure entered the house, carrying a box of Serenity's things. "Ren, I know you said you need your space to clear your head, but I called to make sure you was ok. When you didn't reply to my text, I had to come check on you and bring you your stuff. And don't get mad but I told..." Before Treasure could finish, there was another knock at the door.

"I told Markieff to check on you too. That should be him and Lamont. I thought Aaron might have come home and y'all got into it. You had me scared girl," Treasure informed her.

"It's cool." Serenity smiled. She then got up and answered the door.

"Yo, the fuck wrong with you not answering your phone? Mr. B on the way over too. You got everybody worried and shit. You good? That nigga touch you?" Markieff gave Serenity a once over, making sure she didn't have any marks on her.

"Call my dad and tell him I'm fine. I broke my phone and just didn't feel like getting another one." Serenity told him.

"Ard. Mont, we good. This punk ass not here." Markieff stepped outside and called Benny.

Egypt stood up and grabbed her bag. "Well since you're good, I'm going home. See you tomorrow."

"Really Egypt? I just told you my problem and you're going to leave? At a time like this, I need my big sister's shoulder to fucking cry on, but your selfish ass running out on me. How many times was I there for you when Darren's ass was out slipping and sliding all over Philly with his baby mama. I was there for you. But you know what, fuck you Egypt. You letting whatever happened between you and Shanita fuck up our relationship, is on you. I'm so fucking over your ass right now." Serenity snapped.

"Ren, it's not like…" Egypt started to say but was interrupted when Aaron's best friend Calvin walked in.

Calvin walked in and looked around. Markieff and Lamont was hot on this tail, needing to know who he was.

"Serenity, who the fuck is this funny looking nigga, walking up in here like he pays the bills." Lamont scowled at Calvin.

Calvin sized Lamont up and then did the same with Markieff. He ignored them both and turned back to Serenity. "Aaron sent me over to check on you. He said he haven't heard from you all day. You good?"

"Yep," Serenity answered in a nonchalant tone.

"You sure?" Calvin doubled checked.

"Nigga, she said she was good. Damn," Lamont scoffed.

Serenity didn't want anything to pop off, so she quickly intervened. "Calvin, tell your friend I'm just fine. I'm not trying to be rude, but y'all can go. I'm good."

"Nah, I'm not going anywhere until we talk," Markieff hissed. He then pushed his way inside and sat down on the couch, making himself comfortable.

"Ugh, Markieff..." Serenity started to sigh.

"Kill that noise Lucky, I'm staying. The rest of y'all can go so we can talk."

Calvin stepped inside the house and had to say his piece. "I don't know who you are, but you're not staying nowhere. Her husband not home and you're damn sure not about to be chilling in here."

"Yo, who gave this Buckwheat looking nigga permission to get tough?" Lamont sneered.

"Who the fuck you think you playing with?" Calvin snarled, getting up in Lamont's face.

Lamont stepped back and reached inside his pocket. He pulled out a stick of gum and reached out to Calvin. "Word of advice, make sure your breath not humming when you get in people face."

Calvin smacked Lamont's hand down and turned to Serenity. "Who the fuck are these clown ass niggas? You better let them know I'm not one to play with."

"And neither am I." Lamont shot back. "Kieff, I'm gone man. I'm not trying to catch a charge for this nigga. I got better shit to do. You good here?"

"Yea, I'm good." Markieff answered.

"Come on Treasure, so you can feed me." Lamont said, pulling her hand.

"I guess I will go now." Egypt said.

Serenity let out a snicker. "Sure you are."

Egypt didn't even comment. She pulled Calvin's hand and dragged him down the steps with her. Serenity slammed the door closed, forgetting that quick that Markieff was still there.

"Markieff, I appreciate you checking on me, but I really need to be alone right now."

Markieff got up and walked over to Serenity. He placed his hand underneath her chin, lifting her head. "You sure? It's no problem for me to stay."

"I'm sure. I just need another day, ok."

"Ard." Markieff leaned over, kissing Serenity's forehead.

Why did he do that. Serenity's knees almost buckled beneath her. This was exactly why she couldn't be around him. Her nightly dreams was starting to be nonstop and him being in her presence wasn't helping. She closed her eyes in hopes that when she opened them he was gone, just like in her dreams. But, this wasn't a dream and he wasn't leaving that easily.

"You good? You spaced out on me for a second." Markieff pointed out.

Serenity went to speak, but her words wouldn't come out. Instead, she nodded her head saying yes.

"Good." Markieff pulled her in closer and hugged her tightly. "I will get Kian for you tomorrow and let him chill with me and Mykel. Shana got some act right and letting me get him again. Is that cool with you?"

Again, Serenity nodded her head. For some reason, she couldn't pull her eyes away from Markieff. At that moment, it was like her body had a mind of it's own. Inside, she was screaming, no, don't do that, her hand kept moving up. Markieff stood there looking at her strangely. Serenity got on her tippy toes and her hand finally made it to its destination. She placed it behind his head, pulling him down to her level and kissed his lips. For a second, Markieff was going with the flow, but snapped back into reality when he realized what was happening. He stepped back, and a shocked expression covered his face.

"Yo, what was that about." Markieff asked, licking his lips glad it happened. But, was just a bit curious.

"I...I don't know what came over me. I'm sorry, please lock the door on your way out," Serenity exclaimed, running up the stairs to her room.

Markieff was thrown off from that kiss, but he could feel the sexual tension between them. There was no denying that Markieff was feeling Serenity, but he wasn't going to step to her as a married woman. He didn't even think Serenity looked at him that way, but from that kiss he knew she did. He tucked his bottom lip knowing he had to fight for what he wanted, especially since Aaron didn't appreciate what he had. As much as he wanted to stay, he respected Serenity's wishes and locked the door behind him as he left.

Upstairs, Serenity stood in her bedroom window and watched as Markieff pulled out her driveway. She had never been so confused in her life and hated this feeling. When she kissed Markieff she felt that spark she felt the first time they ever kissed. Aaron has never made her feel that way, not even when they first met.

"Ugh, I should have let him stay," she mumbled to herself.

Chapter 12

It was now Friday, and Markieff felt he had given Serenity enough time to get her mind right. He had so much he needed to talk to her about, including the kiss they shared a few nights ago. Thanks to Kian, he found out what really had Serenity wanting to be alone. Because of that, he was ready to body Aaron for being so damn stupid. It was time she handled her business. She been going through a lot worrying herself over Aaron and enough was enough. Serenity had some life changing decisions to make and he was going to make sure he was there for her when she did.

"Dad, you cooking us breakfast?" Mykel came in the room killing Markieff's thoughts.

"Yea, yea. Give me a minute. Matter of fact go plug up the waffle maker and start the mix for me. I will be down in a minute." Markieff instructed. Reaching across his bed, he grabbed his phone. He was able to talk Serenity into getting a new phone, but she was only taking calls from Kian. He sent her a text, telling her good morning like any other morning.

Then he thought about what today was. He called Treasure hoping she answered. She didn't pick up so he called the one person he knew was close by her.

"Nigga, if she didn't answer, you already knew what time it was. Now you fucking up my groove." Lamont yelled into the phone.

"Oh shut the fuck up and give Treasure the phone with your pressed ass." Markieff laughed.

"I'm not pressed."

Treasure came on the line laughing. "I'm glad somebody knows this boy pressed. But, what's up?"

"I need you to get your girl out that damn house today. Fuck the phone calls, go over and drag her ass out. It's her birthday and I don't want her in that house another day stressing over that bitch made nigga. She doesn't know I know about that picture his side bitch sent and that Kian seen it."

"Yea, I'm sure her ass needs that hair of hers done. Don't worry, I'm on it. I haven't talked to her since that night we all went to check on her. But, I will make sure she comes out and play today."

"Ard. Bring her by the shop over on Sixty-Ninth street and I will give y'all some cash. Everything on me today." Markieff said.

"Oh shit, you're treating me too?" Treasure excitedly asked.

"Like hell. You better ask that nigga next to you." Markieff laughed before hanging up. He got up from the bed and headed downstairs with the boys. He could hear them talking and stopped in his tracks, listening to the conversation between the boys.

"I think my dad like your mom. Hey, you know if they get married, we will be brothers for real." Mykel said.

"I know. But, my mom and dad have to get a divorce first. I just want my mother happy. My dad don't make her happy anymore. I think it's my fault because I told her about the picture. I haven't been home since." Kian told Mykel.

"Damn," Markieff mumbled to himself hearing Kian's little voice. He cleared his throat making his presence known, getting the boys attention.

"Hey dad, we already started the waffles." Mykel told him.

"I see." Markieff glanced over to Kian and it was killing him, seeing him pouting. He pulled out his chair and sat next to Kian. "What's wrong?"

"Nothing," Kian sighed.

"Ki, it's me. Tell Unk what's going on."

"I miss my mother. I know I talked to her, but I want to see her. Today her birthday."

"Call her. After school, we all can go out to eat for her day."

"I will like that. I know she will too. She likes going out." Kian finally smiled.

"I know she does. Come on, let's eat so I can get y'all out of here for school."

The boys quickly ate their breakfast. Markieff made sure he had everything he needed and got the boys out the house. They made it to school in the nick of time. After dropping the boys off, Markieff had a meeting to attend. Benny called him telling him he had some people wanting to buy two of the barbershops. Walking to the front desk, Markieff stood waiting for the lady to lift her head from her phone and acknowledge him. After a second of waiting, he cleared his throat to get her attention. Her head quickly popped up and her phone went down.

"Welcome to Peterson and Thomas, how can I help you." She smiled.

"Hi, I'm here to see Mr. Peterson."

"What's your name?"

"Markieff Ervin."

She picked up her desk phone and hit a button. "I have a Mr. Ervin here to see Mr. Peterson... Ok, I will let him know." She then hung up the phone and smiled at Markieff. "He's on the way down. You can have a seat over there."

"Thank you." Markieff walked over to the chairs in the lobby and took a seat. The front doors opened, causing his attention to shift that way.

"Welcome back Mr. Beal," the receptionist greeted Aaron as he entered the building.

"Thank you Danetta. Is Mr. Peterson in?"

"Yes, but he's about to go out for coffee with this gentleman." Danetta smiled at Markieff.

Aaron clenched his jaws, giving Markieff a smug look. The elevator door opened and Mr. Peterson stepped off. Markieff stood to his feet and fixed his jacket.

"Mr. Peterson, do you need me to go with you?" Aaron asked.

"No, I'm sure I can handle this one. You had the opportunity to close this deal, but you didn't. Danetta, please hold all my calls until I get back."

Seeing the disappointment covering Aaron's face was pure satisfaction to Markieff. Benny told him that most likely Aaron was the one calling the meeting, but Markieff made sure he wasn't. Especially since he was supposed to still be out of town.

***

Aaron rushed upstairs and headed straight to James' office, slamming the door shut. When he slammed it, he shattered the glass.

James jumped out his seat. "You just broke my fucking door. The fuck wrong with you?"

"I didn't mean for that to happen." Aaron sighed.

James shook his head disgusted. He picked up his desk phone and called the maintenance man to come clean up the glass. He then packed up his stuff and went to Aaron's office.

"You care to tell me what your problem is this morning?" James asked, sitting at the other end of Aaron's desk.

"You knew Peterson's ugly ass had a meeting this morning with Markieff?"

"Yea, you didn't?" James raised his brows.

"Nah. Fuck it, I'm glad I don't have to beg that nigga for shit." Aaron scoffed.

"Umm hmm. But yo, where the hell you sleep for the last two days? I know your ass didn't go home yet." James pointed out.

"I got a room. I didn't want to go until tonight. You know after what Calvin told me, I'm going to come clean and tell Serenity everything and beg for forgiveness."

"Man just do her a favor and leave. Coming clean is not going to do shit. Nigga, it would be different if you fucked a random, but you didn't. You really think she will forgive and forget after that."

"Damn, who side you on Jay. You supposed to be giving me words of encouragement."

"What's encouraging about this shit you got going on? I'm keeping it real with you. Shit, you better be thinking about what Mr. Benny's going to do to your ass when he gets wind of this shit. Told you to leave Nene ass alone a long time ago, and Egypt, you shouldn't have even gone there. If I was their father, I would kill you boy."

Aaron slammed his back on his chair. "Fuck, I forgot about Mr. Benny."

"I know you did."

"Ard, maybe I will hold off on that. Don't worry, tonight I will make it up to her. I'm not going to call her today. Let her think I forgot. So, when she gets home, she will be shocked from all the stuff I have planned for her." Aaron beamed.

"Ok. Hopefully this bullshit plan works." James laughed.

"You know what, fuck you and all this negative energy you got. I got this." Aaron said, hoping his plan would work too. Saying it out loud, made him realize he might not be able to pull this off since he hasn't heard from Serenity. "Bruh, I'm a bit surprised Serenity haven't called me nagging about not calling her."

"Oh really. She hasn't called you since you left? Not even after that night you sent Calvin over there?" James questioned.

"Nope."

"Dude, you're in trouble."

"How you figure?"

"Bruh, when a woman is nagging as you call it, she's doing it for a reason. Let me put it like this, she knows when you got another female auditioning for her spot. They fuss because they fighting to keep that number one spot. When she stop all that, her silence means she about to leave your black ass. That's when you know another nigga is out here doing what you're not, giving her attention."

Aaron let James' words sink in. The thought crossed his mind a few times about Serenity cheating with Markieff. At that thought, he knew he couldn't tell Serenity the truth and risk losing her to another man. Instead, he was going to do right and fight for his.

"Got you thinking huh?" James teased.

Aaron kissed his teeth. "No. I just can't see Serenity doing me wrong. She wants what her parents have, and that's a long marriage." Aaron said, more so to convince himself that it was a true statement.

"Like I said before, that rabbit got that gun locked and loaded." James laughed.

Aaron brushed off what James was saying. He wasn't trying to think about what he was saying. He was going to think positive and just knew he could fix his situation. Just as the thought crossed his mind, his phone buzzed. There wasn't no need to look down, because only one person would be calling that phone.

"See, your ass can't do right. Why you still have that phone if you supposed to had cut Nene off. Bruh, you don't have to lie to me, I know that's where you been the last two nights."

"Ard yea, I was over there. Had to take one more ride before I cut her all the way off. It wasn't easy, but I think she's good now. I'm not going to have any problems out of her."

"You get dumb and dumber by the second. Man, I'm going to work from the conference room. You're terrible bruh. I will pray for you. For real for real."

"Fuck you Jay. But yo, you can stay. I'm taking the rest of the day off. I'm going to get everything ready at home." Aaron smiled to himself, thinking about how he was going to have the house covered from wall to wall with gifts.

****

Serenity and Treasure was sitting in the waiting area of the nail shop, waiting their turn.

"Ugh, I don't know why I let you drag me out the house. I don't feel like being around anybody."

Serenity whined. She picked up her phone for the hundredth time, checking it.

"Oh hush that shit up. It's your day girl. We about to turn the fuck up. You been in that damn house long enough."

"Whatever hoe," Serenity laughed. "Hold up, how you get a Friday off?"

"I called in sick. I might not be going back. Markieff wants me to come work with him. I don't know why you don't come too." Treasure said.

"Shit, I just might now. Now that I'm jobless." Serenity said picking up her phone again.

"Why you keep looking at your phone? Who you waiting on to call you?"

"You know Aaron didn't even call me this morning. It's my birthday and the least this nigga could do is call. Even if I'm mad at his ass."

"Humph, fuck him. Another reason why you need to turn the fuck up tonight."

"You know what, you're right. After this, let's go shopping for a new outfit. Shit, it's been a minute since I been to a club. Tonight, we going."

"Yesss. One time for the birthday bitch," Treasure sung as she danced in her seat. Her phone went off and she quickly answered it. "Yes sir."

"Where y'all at? I told Kian we was taking Serenity to lunch today. I'm headed to the school to get him out early."

"We getting our nails done right now."

"Bet, bring her to D&B. I will get a back room closed off for us. Plus, Kian suggested it. He just wants to see Serenity smile."

"Aww, that's so sweet. Ok, I will make that happen. I will text you when we done." Treasure ended the call in the nick of time. Two chairs was free and they was next up.

They walked over to the chairs and sat down. Treasure could feel Serenity's eyes on her and tried to ignore her.

"Umm, who was you on the phone with?" Serenity asked.

"Ugh, nosey, aren't we?" Treasure joked with a slight giggle.

"Was that your new boo Lamont?" Serenity smirked. "I peeped that shit the other night at my house. I might have been in my little mood, but I saw that shit between you two. So, when did that shit start?"

Treasure playfully rolled her eyes. "Ugh, it's nothing. He slid in my inbox one night. I thought it was kind of cute how he did it. We went out for drinks and shit, my ass wanted to see if his ass could back up all that mouth he got about his stroke game. I have to say, shorty got skills," Treasure started dancing in her seat.

"Eww, you could have left that part out." Serenity laughed. "I'm glad you gave him a chance. I really think he's a good dude. Just needed a good woman to tame his ass."

"We just chilling for now. He is cool once you get to know him." Treasure smiled.

"Thank you for this. I really did need to get my ass out the house."

"I know this."

"You make me sick. Before we go shopping, let's grab something to eat. I'm hungry as hell."

"Yea, I was just thinking about that." Treasure smirked.

"Remind me to text my sister and cousin. I want to invite them out tonight. Although I'm pissed at my sister, I still want them to celebrate my day with me."

"I don't care for your damn cousin. Especially since I know she friends with Toni ass."

"Ugh, I forgot all about that shit," Serenity scoffed.

The girls talked more, and Treasure filled Serenity in on a few things. Serenity was thankful for the much needed time out the house. For the first time in days, she wasn't stressing over Aaron and what he was doing. Right after the nail salon, Treasure drove over to Dave & Busters. She texted Markieff, letting him know they were on the way.

"I know damn well you didn't bring me here for lunch." Serenity frowned up her face.

"What's wrong with here? I need one of those Original Coronaritas and that damn salmon."

"They do have some good salmon." Serenity agreed.

Getting out the car, they walked inside. Markieff already told Treasure where to find them. She then led Serenity to the party room. Serenity wasn't even paying attention. She was too busy with her phone. When the doors opened, Serenity's head quickly popped up.

"Surprise," everyone yelled.

Serenity's mouth hung opened. Tears of joy started rolling down her face. She damn sure wasn't excepting this. Kian came up to her and hugged her.

"Happy birthday mommy."

"Thank you, baby," Serenity kissed his forehead. She looked around the room and couldn't believe it. It was decked out with red and white balloons.

"You like it mommy?" Kian asked.

"No, I love it baby."

Serenity looked around the room and smiled at Mr. Benny. "Thank you, daddy."

Benny shook his head. "Oh no sweetheart. I had no dealings with this. This all Markieff's doing."

Serenity's head quickly whipped around and faced Markieff. "You did this?"

"I did, but it was Kian's idea. He wanted to see his mommy smile for her birthday." Markieff informed her.

Kian was still hugging Serenity. She then hugged him tighter. "Thank you, baby boy. Mommy love you so much." Serenity fought back her tears. She had mixed emotions. She was glad Markieff was able to help Kian with making her day a good day, but it should have been Aaron that helped their son bring a smile to her face. Stepping out of her embrace with Kian, she went over to Markieff.

"Thank you sooo much," Serenity stressed, hugging him.

Markieff wrapped his arms around her waist. "You're welcome." Serenity pulled back and looked him in his eyes. The lust filled in her stare told him everything he needed to know about how she felt about him. He leaned in closer and whispered in her ear. "If you don't want me to bend your ass over and give you something real, you better let go."

Serenity stepped back and playfully hit his chest. "Ugh, you got jokes. Always gotta find a way to fuck up the moment. You play too much," she giggled.

Markieff winked and grabbed her hand. He led her over to the table and pulled out her chair. "Have a seat birthday girl." Once Serenity was seated, Markieff leaned over and whispered in her ear again. "F.Y.I, I wasn't joking. Yo, somebody get the waitress. I'm hungry as hell." He yelled after kissing the side of Serenity's neck.

Serenity couldn't contain the smile that spread across her face. She didn't think her birthday was going to be a good one, but things was turning out to be great. It wasn't nothing major, but the simple and small things like this meant a lot to her. The fact that it was Kian's idea made it better. At this point, she didn't even care that Aaron hasn't called yet. Moments later, to her surprise Egypt and her boyfriend came walking in. Egypt walked up and Serenity could have sworn she spotted tears in her eyes.

"Happy birthday sis. I'm sorry for acting like a selfish bitch." Egypt admitted.

"Thank you."

"We need to talk. I...I know who..." Egypt started to say.

"Listen, I don't even care right now. Let me enjoy my day and worry about other shit later. Now, let's eat."

Everyone had ordered their food and was enjoying themselves. After eating her food, Serenity went to play games with Kian. Her phone was going dead, so she just turned it off. Far as she was concerned, everyone that mattered to her was helping her celebrate her day.

"Lucky, let's see who got the better shot," Markieff said, opening up a challenge.

"You're on. What we playing for?"

Markieff shrugged his shoulders. "I don't know, what you want."

"You," she thought to herself. Instead, she said, "Loser pays for drinks tonight."

"Oh, we partying tonight?" Markieff raised his brows.

"Well, it was going to be just me and the girls, but you're more than welcome to join us."

"Bet," Markieff agreed.

For another hour, Serenity enjoyed the first half of the birthday celebration with her family. Once they was finished at Dave and Busters, she and Treasure headed to the mall to find something to wear for the club. Then, they stopped at the hair salon to get their hair done. At this point, Serenity was ready to throw in the towel and go home and get in the bed.

"Girl, I don't even know if I can make it out tonight. My ass truly is getting old." Serenity blurted out.

"Umm, no ma'am. It's still early. We can go to my house, take a little nap until nine then hit the club." Treasure suggested.

"Ok, that might just work." With that, Serenity was ready. They headed to Treasure's house and

Serenity went straight to the guest room. Soon as she hit the bed, she fell asleep.

Chapter 13

Aaron was home getting the house ready for Serenity. He had done bought at least fifty balloons to fly high around the house. He had every color of roses spread around the house. Now, he was in the kitchen finishing up dinner.

"Anything else you need done bruh?" James asked.

Aaron took a second and looked around. "Nah, I think this is it."

"Ard. I'm out, it's a big party tonight at Vanity Grand. Calvin got one of the Skyboxes for us."

"Damn, I wish I could roll. But, I gotta do this."

"You damn sure do. Hit my line in the morning and let me know how that shit turn out." James gave Aaron brotherly hug and made his exit.

Aaron checked the time and saw it was getting close to when Serenity usually gets home. He still doesn't know about her getting fired since they haven't talked to each other. He did a final once over and smiled to himself. The ringing of his phone knocked him out of his thoughts. Taking out his phone his brows raised not recognizing the number, but he should have.

"Hello."

"Damn, you're still alive I see. You must haven't told wifey about us yet."

"What the fuck you doing calling this phone. I told you last night I was done, for good this time Nene." Aaron snarled.

"Oh I know, and I believe you. But I know you will be back soon as wifey puts your ass out. I was just checking to see what time you will be home baby. I was thinking about going out tonight and wanted you to know I wouldn't be home when you got here." Nene laughed into the phone.

Aaron didn't even respond as he ended the call. Going back into the kitchen, he turned off the stove. Everything was ready and now just waiting for Serenity to come home. He ran upstairs and started her bath. Taking one of the roses, he peeled off the petals dropping them into the water. Getting a few candles, he lit them and placed them around the tub.

Going back into the bedroom, Aaron laid on the bed with a wide smile. He knew Serenity was going to be happy once she saw everything he did. She was romantic and loved stuff like this. It's been a while since Aaron done something like this and he was glad he did it at a time he felt was right. Checking the time again, he was surprised she wasn't home yet. Picking up his phone he tried calling her, but her phone was going straight to voicemail.

"Not this shit again," Aaron mumbled to himself. He left a voicemail, asking her about her whereabouts and what time she was coming home. Purposely, he didn't tell her happy birthday. He was going to wait to see her to tell her that.

***

"It was now nine-fifteen and Treasure was trying to wake Serenity up.

"Ren, get your ass up girl," Treasure shook her.

"Ugh, I'm up." Serenity grunted.

"Wipe your mouth with all that damn drool."

"Shut up, shit. That sleep was good." Serenity laughed, wiping her mouth.

SOUL Publications

"I bet it was. Umm, missy you have explaining to do too."

Serenity tilted her head and said, "I do?"

"Yes. Bitch, you was in here moaning Markieff's damn name."

Serenity's hands quickly covered her mouth as a shocked expression painted her face. "Are you serious?"

"Yes ma'am. So spill it. You two fucked?"

"No fool, I'm still a married woman. Despite what I think my husband is doing, I wouldn't."

"Fuck that marriage. Clearly you're with the wrong man. Plus, I saw the way you looked at that man today. Hell, even the way he looks at you tells how he really feel. If you ask me, I don't think he ever looked at you as a sister. Maybe you was just to young to understand, but I feel that man always loved you more than a friend." Treasure pointed out.

Serenity bit the fold of her cheeks to stop herself from smiling. After the way Markieff's been coming at her, she was starting to think the same thing and wished she would have known this before he moved away.

"Look at this. This is pure love in you twos eyes." Treasure held her phone out in front of Serenity, showing her a picture she took of her and Markieff earlier.

"This is a cute picture. Send it to me please."

"Can I post this on my page."

Serenity smirked. "You petty as hell, but I don't even care. Let me go take a shower and get dressed. I'm ready to party now." Serenity started dancing around.

"Yesss, go best friend, that's my best friend." Treasure started singing and dancing along with Serenity.

"You so damn silly."

"I already took my shower while you was sleep. So, hurry up. I only have to touch up my makeup and I will be ready."

"Ard."

With that, Serenity jetted to the bathroom. She was excited to go out and have some fun with her girls. Then, Markieff crossed her mind causing her to smile hard. She quickly took a shower and got dressed.

"How I look?" Serenity asked, turning around for Treasure to get a full view of her outfit.

"You look cute bestie." Treasure complimented. "Has Aaron called yet?" she curiously questioned.

"Oh shit, I turned my phone off when we were at Dave and Busters because it was going dead. You got a charger because I left my shit at home."

"Girl really. You know I'm team iPhone."

"Damn. Well, let me turn it on and if the bitch goes dead, oh well." Walking out the room, Serenity went to retrieve her phone. She got it and turned it on. She went back into Treasure's room and plopped down on the bed. Soon as it was powered on, her messages popped up.

"Humph, the nigga did call," she said out loud, listening to Aaron's message. Once it was done, she frowned up her face.

"What?" Treasure asked out of concern.

"This nigga still hasn't told me happy birthday. He is asking me what time I was coming home. I wonder if he's home?"

"Girl, fuck Aaron. Tonight, we not thinking about him. Hurry up and finish getting ready, so we can go." Treasure ordered.

"Yes mother," Serenity laughed.

An hour later, the ladies was ready and finally leaving out the door. Serenity sent Shanita a text telling her she was welcome to come join them tonight and informed her that Egypt was going to be there. She then called Kian to tell him goodnight.

"Hey mommy." Kian beamed with excitement.

"Hey baby. I was calling to thank you again for getting everyone together for my birthday. I had so much fun with you. And maybe tomorrow, we can go to the movies or something." Treasure suggested.

"Ok. Mom, I'm not trying to rush you or anything, but me and Mykel in the middle of a match."

"Really, you don't want to talk to me?"

"I mean, I do but..." Kian started to say.

"I'm messing with you baby. Goodnight. Oh, tell your grandmother my phone is going dead so I'm turning it off and to call Auntie Treasure phone if she needs me."

"Got it. Is that it?" Kian eagerly asked.

"Bye Ki."

With that, Kian hung up. Serenity shook her head with a smile on her face. Her baby boy was growing up. Pulling up to the club, they saw the line was wrapped around the building. They didn't realize it was a big party tonight for the reunion tour of State Property.

"Girl, this shit is packed," Serenity said.

"Sure is. Don't worry, Markieff said we got a skybox. He called and pulled some strings to get one for us."

"Skybox?"

"Right, you haven't been here. Yea, it's the upstairs VIP section. They have two levels and this place be litty."

Once inside, Serenity's eyes grew big. "Bitch, this a strip club?"

"Duh. I need for you to get out more. Married to that square, your ass forgot how to have fun I see."

"Shut up," Serenity pushed Treasure.

They bopped their way though the crowd as they headed to their section. Markieff, Lamont and two other guys was already seated, with a few dancers giving them a lap dance.

"Ayee, turn up," Treasure yelled.

Markieff stood to his feet and hugged Serenity once she was close. "Fix your face. Matter fact take a shot and loosen up. Tonight, I'm going to bring out my Lucky."

"Oh really?" Serenity teased.

"Yes, really. T, pour your girl two shots. She got some catching up to do.

Treasure did as she was told and fixed herself and Serenity's drinks. She handed Serenity her glass while she held hers in the air.

"Cheers to the birthday bitch," Treasure cheered.

They clicked glasses and grabbed the second shot, taking it to the head.

"That's my Lucky," Markieff smiled. "T, fix another round," he smiled.

Serenity shook her head, knowing Markieff was going to have her drunk as hell by the end of the night. She wasn't complaining not one bit, but she knew once she gets to that point, it was no telling what she would do after.

"Girl, you see this?" Treasure asked, pointing towards the door. "Your cousin foul. She knows you don't fuck with that bitch Toni and still comes in here with her. That bitch can't sit with us." Treasure snarled.

Shanita came up to the section and left Toni and their other friends at the bar.

"Happy birthday cousin." Shanita said to Serenity.

"Thank you. What's up with the extra company?"

"You didn't get my message. When you texted me, I was already with Toni. We just coming back from Jersey and she wanted to come. I was trying to get her to take me home..." Shanita started to explain.

"Girl, it's cool. Go have fun with your girls." Serenity smiled.

"You sure?"

"Yes."

Shanita gave Serenity a hug and headed back down to the bar.

"I don't like that chick. It's just something about her that don't sit to well with me. The fact that she's cool with the enemy doesn't help. I can understand why Egypt stop fucking with her ass." Treasure pointed out.

"What about me?" Egypt asked, walking up on them.

"About time you made it. I was starting to think you wasn't going to come." Serenity said.

"I told you I was." Egypt hugged Serenity. She sat next to her and looked out at the crowd on the lower level. Her eyes connected with Shanita and she let out a snicker. "Why your favorite cousin not up here with you?"

"Not tonight." Serenity quickly warned her, shutting down whatever she was trying to start.

"Damn, I was just asking a question, but ok."

Serenity dismissed Egypt's last comment and went back to enjoying her night. After six shots of Patron, she was starting to feel the effects and it even gave her some confidence.

The crew was going hard having a good time. Egypt was surprised to see Serenity coming out of her shell. She was up dancing and what happen next surprised everyone. Serenity was standing in front of Markieff and started to slow wine her hips. At this point, all eyes was on them, including some extra ones.

Markieff sat up and grabbed Serenity by her hips, pulling her down on his lap. "Yo, don't do no shit like that teasing a nigga," he warned her.

Serenity smirked as she stood up and turned to face him. She then pushed him back and straddled his lap. She bit down on her bottom lip as she started slowly grinding on his growing manhood.

"Maybe I want to start something." Serenity shot back.

Sitting up again, Markieff wrapped his arms around her. "As bad as I want to bend your ass over and fuck you into submission, I'm going to wait. Right now, you're drunk and I don't want no drunk pussy and you regret doing the shit in the morning. So, we will revisit this conversation on a later day. With that being said, get up before you give a nigga blue balls."

Grinding on him for a second more, Serenity smirked before leaning forward. "Who said I would regret it?" She whispered in his ear. Kissing his cheek, she finally got up and sat next to Treasure.

"Girl, I know I said turn up, but damn." Treasure exclaimed.

"Just having a little fun. You only live once right? Plus, I see his punk ass homeboys over there staring. They can go run and tell that shit." Serenity smirked.

"Right," Treasure laughed.

"What time is it?" Serenity asked.

"Almost three in the morning," Egypt answered.

"I'm ready to go. I don't think I can hang until four." Serenity yawned.

"Well, you can stay with me," Treasure suggested.

"Umm, no. I see how Lamont looking at you. Girl, you can take me home and let that man get some cutty." Serenity laughed.

Markieff walked over and wrapped his arms over Serenity's shoulders. He whispered something in her ear, causing her to smile from ear to ear. He then kissed the back of her neck, sending chills though her body. She looked up and saw that spark in his eyes that Treasure mentioned. She knew if she went home with him, she was no better than Aaron for cheating. She was going to do things right and once Aaron got home, they was going to have a long talk.

Since Egypt didn't have that much to drink, she was the one to take Serenity home. Treasure offered, but Serenity declined, knowing Lamont was trying to get in her pants. Although she didn't want to, she said her goodbyes to Markieff. After the day they had, she knew things between them wasn't going to be the same. From the kiss they shared, she knew they had true feeling for each other.

On the car ride home Serenity was in deep thought. She had some serious decisions to make and had to do it soon. She knew she and Aaron had grown apart and his cheating didn't help. She always thought she would fight for her marriage, but now she wasn't so sure. Markieff came in and didn't make things any better. Closing her eyes Serenity drifted off to sleep for the rest of the ride.

***

Back at the house, Aaron was fuming with anger. He had been sitting in the house for hours waiting for Serenity. He even fell asleep and still no Serenity. But, that wasn't why he was pissed. His jaws clenched as he watched the video of Serenity grinding on Markieff. Nene sent him the video an hour ago throwing it in his face. He could hear Serenity at the door fumbling to unlock it. He tossed his phone on the coffee table and sat back, waiting for her to enter.

Serenity finally got the door opened and stumbled into the house.

"Had fun?" Aaron sarcastically asked.

Startled, Serenity jumped back holding her chest. "Damn, you scared the shit out of me. What are you doing here?"

"I fucking live here. Answer my question, did you have fun."

"Sure did. I guess your brother sent you pictures of me enjoying my birthday that you failed to even acknowledge."

Aaron got up and turned on the lights. "Happy fucking birthday. I didn't tell you because I had plans to surprise you. But like always, you fucked that up by not coming home or even answering my fucking calls."

Serenity looked around the house and wasn't even impressed. She rolled her eyes. "Ok thank you, I guess. But you said you wasn't even going to be here so I wasn't trying to be in the house on my day. Sue me for wanting to have a good time." Serenity then started up the steps.

"Going to wash that nigga off you?" Aaron blurted out.

Stopping dead in her tracks, Serenity looked over the rail. "Excuse me?"

"I didn't fucking stutter."

"I mean, I have to wash right?"

"So, you going to stand there and admit you fucked that nigga?"

Serenity knew she could have cleared the air right then and there, but didn't want to. She wanted Aaron to do the worrying for once. She wanted him to feel what she been feeling these few months.

"Aaron, I'm not in the mood for your theatrics right now. We can talk in the morning because at this point, it's much needed."

"Nah, we talking now. Did you fuck that nigga?" Aaron snarled.

Serenity slowly turned around. "I said I'm not in the mood to talk about this."

"It's either yes or no."

"Ok, you want to talk, let's talk. Did you fuck that bitch that sent you the nude picture to your phone that our son seen? Tell me, did you Aaron?"

Aaron's mouth formed the letter O, not sure what to say.

Serenity chuckled. "Thought so. Like I said, we can talk in the fucking morning. Don't come at me when you're out here doing your fucking dirt. So, go ahead and sit there and think about how you're going to lie your way out this shit, because that's all you're going to do. Oh, and stay your ass down here. I would like to sleep alone like I been doing."

Aaron still was sitting there in silence. He knew Kian was going to out him sooner or later. Picking up his phone, he called James. He answered on the second ring.

"Yea," James dryly answered.

"Bruh, she knows. Kian told her about the pictures."

"As he should."

"What? What you mean as he should? Damn, who side you're on?"

"The right side. Shit, I feel sorry for you bruh. That nigga Markieff was doing something I haven't seen you do for Serenity in a minute." James teased.

"Yea, what's that trader?"

"Smile."

"Hold up, you saw her at the club tonight and didn't do shit? What type of shit you on? Where does your loyalty lie?" Aaron scoffed.

"Look, I told you to do right by that girl. Why should I out her when I didn't out you? What y'all do is y'all business, not mine."

"I'm starting to feel like you want my wife." Aaron speculated.

"Good night Aaron," James said, hanging up.

Aaron tossed his phone on the table, not believing James' attitude. He laid back, seething with anger over this whole situation. The shoe was now on the other foot and he was seeing Karma coming his way. The thought of losing Serenity never crossed his mind until now. He really thought they could kiss and make up and everything could go back to normal. Closing his eyes, Aaron decided to go to sleep. It wasn't no need to think of a lie because he was going to come clean.

The next day, Aaron was awakened by his ringing phone. He reached over and grabbed it from the table. When he saw who it was, he tossed his phone back on the table. He sat up and ran his hands over his face. He knew this conversation between him and Serenity wasn't going to go over so well. Getting up, he headed upstairs. When he got to the room Serenity was still sleep. He went into the bathroom to use it. As he was relieving himself, he could hear Serenity moaning. He licked his lips thinking pleasing her body would help their conversation go over well. Going over to the bed he got in trying not to make his presence known just yet. Once he was safely in the bed he wrapped his arms around Serenity and rubbed his hands across her breasts. He kissed her neck causing her to moan, but what she moaned wasn't anything he wanted to hear.

"Umm, just like that Markieff." Serenity moaned.

Aaron jumped out the bed seething with anger. Serenity didn't even budge. Her hand was still down her pants as it moved faster up and down. He couldn't believe she was masturbating thinking about the next man. His jaws clenched, and he just stood there and watched. He wanted to see her face once she woke up from her dream. She got louder and he could only wonder if she was doing this on purpose. Could she had felt him getting in the bed and messing with his mental? If she was, it damn sure was working.

"Fuuccckk," Serenity sung as her body jerked. Her eyes slowly opened and again, she was startled. "What the fuck, why are you just standing there like some creep," she fussed getting out the bed.

"Was it good?" Aaron asked, following her into the bathroom.

"Was what good?" Serenity played stupid. She knew what he was talking about seeing that he was standing over. What she didn't know is that she moaned Markieff's name out loud for him to hear.

"That wet dream you was having about that nigga. Your so-called homie."

"Boy, nobody was having a wet dream."

"You yelled his fucking name when I touched you," Aaron screamed. "So like I asked you last night, did you fuck that nigga?"

Serenity didn't answer him. She walked back into the room and sat down on the bed and crossed her arms over her chest. "Did you fuck that girl in the picture?"

"Yes," Aaron admitted.

Serenity gasped for air, hearing him finally admitting to cheating. She closed her eyes and snickered. She thought tears was forming but they didn't. Him telling the truth didn't hurt her like she thought it would have.

"So, this shit makes us even. I don't even care if you fucked him. Now we both did something and we can kiss and make up now. I'm sorry for what I did and I promise I'm done with her. She didn't mean shit to me," Aaron ranted.

"Even? This makes us even. Really nigga? First off, I didn't fuck Markieff. Lawd knows I should have, but I'm not you. Yes, I was wrong for kissing him, but that is all that happened between us. You on the other hand out here fucking bitches like I'm not taking care of home."

"Ren, for a minute you weren't. There is no excuse for what I did. I was wrong and I will own up to that. I just want to move on from this and work on us."

"I don't." Serenity blurted out.

"What you mean, you don't?"

"I think we need some time apart. I remember the first time I asked you about cheating. You asked me why was I still here if I felt you was cheating right? Now that you just admitted to it, I want to weigh out my options."

Aaron chuckled. "Weigh out your options huh?" Aaron mocked. "This is about you and Markieff right? You got feelings for this nigga right? But sitting here trying to blame me for what's going on." Aaron stated, trying to flip the script.

"Oh boy please, you tried it. Our problems started way before Markieff came into the picture. I knew for a while that you was cheating but couldn't prove that shit. Matter fact since we talking, how long Aaron?"

Aaron ran his hand over his face and gave it some thought. Right now, Serenity didn't know who he was cheating with and that was the only thing that could work in his favor. So, he lied like he been doing.

"Only a few months."

"Who is she?" Serenity continued to question.

"Come on Ren, it doesn't matter, she doesn't matter. She never did. I was stupid and I know that now. She meant nothing to me but a quick fuck."

"You're lying. I know it's been more than a few months. I don't even care about that shit right now. Thank you for admitting to this shit, but I need some time to myself."

"How long?" Aaron sighed.

"I don't know."

"So, you're not even going to fight for our marriage?"

"Nigga, I been fighting. Now, it's your turn. If you really love me I shouldn't have been put in a position to have to fight for shit. You made your bed, now lay in that bitch. Please leave. I have a lot to think about."

Aaron bit down on his bottom lip wanting to say something. Serenity put him in his place, calling him out on his bullshit. Feeling defeated he went over to his closet and grabbed a few outfits. Looking back at Serenity, Aaron didn't have anything else to say. He grabbed the last of his things that was on the floor and looked up at Serenity.

"Ren, I love you."

Serenity sucked her teeth. "Where was that love when you was out fucking other bitches?"

Instead of digging himself deeper in the hole, Aaron turned around and left out like he was asked. He hated to go over to James' house because he knew all he was going to say was, I told you so. Plus, he was still baffled at how James came at him about Serenity. That didn't sit too well with him. Not wanting to be alone he took out his phone and called an old friend.

"Yo, you busy?" He asked.

"Why?"

"I need to talk."

"You need to talk or you want to fuck?"

"Talk man, for real. Your sister just put me out. I told her everything but didn't give no names. I just need that friend that you used to be. Remember how you used to come to me about Darren, well I need that type of shit right now. Please," Aaron begged.

"Ugh, come on." Egypt said, feeling sorry for him.

"Ard, thank you." Aaron looked back at his house and let out a frustrated breath. Serenity made a good point, he made this mess and had to live with the consequences. He just prayed their love was strong enough to get back to how they used to be. He was slowly understanding what James was trying to tell him. The thought of losing Serenity never his mind because Markieff wasn't in the picture to give her an option. Now, he was paying for it.

SOUL Publications

Chapter 14

Serenity was proud of herself. She thought once she found out the truth about Aaron, she would be somewhere balled up in a corner crying her eyes out. Instead, she was out and about living her best life. It was still her birthday weekend and she was going to enjoy it. It was Saturday night and she was out with Shanita. They were sitting at the bar and Serenity was telling her everything that happened with Aaron.

"Girl, I can't believe Aaron. I thought he loved you." Shanita shook her head.

"Yea, me too."

Egypt walked into the bar and Shanita rolled her eyes.

"Your slick ass. You could have told me she was coming." Shanita scoffed.

"I don't know what's wrong between you two, but y'all need to fix that shit now. That's all I want for my birthday."

"Well, tell her that. I told you, I don't even know why she stopped fucking with me."

Egypt walked over to the table with her face frowned up. "Really Serenity?"

"Yes really. You two are too fucking grown to be acting like y'all eighteen. Whatever beef you two have, that shit ends now. I need to go pee, so talk until I get back." Serenity got up from her seat and headed to the bathroom. Her phone rung and a smiled covered her face as she answered.

"Hey you," she beamed.

"Lucky, where you at girl?"

"At Darrius' Bar and Grill with Shanita and Egypt's ass. Where you at?

"Home. I been sleep all damn day. Went over to see your dad and thought Mykel was coming home with me, but he wanted to stay with Ki. I'm in for the night. Man, last night took a lot out of me. I'm getting old." Markieff joked.

"I feel the same way, but wanted to grab something to eat."

"Word, you should be nice and bring your boy something to eat. Plus, I got something for you."

"Ugh, always talking nasty."

"Shit, I wasn't talking about that, so look who's mind in the gutter. I mean I got that too for you, but you're not ready for that shit. Your ass will be headed to divorce court for real." Markieff halfway joked.

"Yea, I might be going there anyways," Serenity sighed.

"What happened?"

"I will tell you when I come over. What you want to eat?"

"Anything. A nigga hungry as hell."

"Ok, got you. See you in a little while. Shit, I got something for your ass to eat," Serenity mumbled placing her phone in her back pocket. She rushed into the restroom before she peed on herself. As she was washing her hands she felt her phone vibrating in her pocket. She pulled it out and read her message from Markieff.

Mar: Learn to properly hang up your phone before talking shit. I done warned you about talking like that. Don't ask for something you're not ready for, because I will eat my way to your heart.

Serenity's mouth hit the floor not believing Markieff heard her. Then her dreams of him eating her out crossed her mind and instantly she felt the heat growing between her legs.

"Get it together Serenity," she coached herself.

When she got back to the table, to her surprise both Shanita and Egypt was still sitting there. Both was on their phones, but at least they wasn't fighting.

"Did we kiss and make up?" Serenity asked, sitting in her seat.

"Yep," Shanita popped her lips. She tossed her phone into her bag and stood to her feet. "Ren, don't think I'm running but my boo just got into town and I haven't seen him in weeks. Enjoy your night." Shanita walked over and hugged Serenity. For show she went over to Egypt and they gave each other a half hug.

"Ard, I'm about to get out of here anyways. Text me when you get home." Serenity told her.

"Ugh really? I just got here and you're leaving me?" Egypt scoffed.

"That's your fault. I been here almost an hour and half waiting for you. Anyways, Markieff called and wanted me to bring him something to eat."

"Umm hmm, what he about eat?" Egypt smirked.

Serenity reached over and hit her arm. "Stop being nasty. You know it's not even like that between us. Plus, I'm still married to that asshole."

Egypt lowered her head feeling bad for being partly the reason her sister was feeling the pain she was. Now that she and Aaron talked, they will take their affair to their graves. She couldn't tell her sister what happened and further hurt her. They even agreed to leave Nene out of it too. Serenity didn't need to know names.

"I know and the hell with him. He did him, so why can't you do you? You kicked him out right? Are you really going to work it out with him?"

Serenity's brows raised. "How you know I kicked him?"

"Fuck," Egypt cursed to herself. "Oh, he called me. He came over to talk and that's partly the reason I was late coming out. He wanted me to talk to you. He was trying to sound all sad and shit but I'm team Serenity. I sat and let his ass vent. I'm not even going to try and talk you into working shit out unless that's what you want to do. Either way, I'm riding with my sister." Egypt quickly covered up her slip up.

"Yea you're right, fuck him. Like for real, why am I thinking about his feelings when he didn't give a fuck about mine. No lie, I been having sexual dreams about Markieff."

Egypt moved her chair closer to the table. "Do tell. Was it good?"

"Girl that's the problem, it was more than good. Hell, Aaron even heard me calling out Markieff's name while I was having a dream. Apparently, I was masturbating and all. As of lately, Markieff's been making me feel a way I never felt with Aaron. Bad thing about it, I don't even think Markieff be trying to do it. He just does it, if that makes sense."

"Yea, it does. Markieff's always been that way. You just never saw it because of how close you two were. That man loves you and I never realized that shit until last night. Ren, Markieff is the man for you. I think he came back at the right time for all the right reasons. Aaron was about to drive your ass crazy and Markieff was here to pick you up."

Serenity couldn't fight back the smile that plastered her face. What Egypt was saying made sense. The waitress came back over to the table and Serenity ordered Markieff's food. Egypt sat with her and they talked a little more.

Serenity arrived to Markieff's house. Out nowhere, she became a ball of nerves. Beads of sweat formed on her forehead and her legs was shaking.

"Ugh, get it together Serenity. This is Markieff," she tried calming herself.

Getting out the car she walked up to the door. Taking a deep breath, she knocked and stepped back.

"It's open fool," Markieff yelled.

Slowly Serenity turned the knob getting herself together. When she walked in Markieff was laying on the couch watching tv. He was so comfortable he didn't even bother to remove his hands from his pants, or try to change the channel he was watching.

"Really Markieff."

Markieff kissed his teeth. "Don't act like you don't watch the playboy channel." He sat up and stood to his feet. "You want to finish the job," he smirked as he stretched his arms.

"Ugh, I don't like you."

"I'm just fucking with you. You can't handle all this dick I got over here," he informed her.

Serenity's eyes traveled down to the center of Markieff's basketball shorts. She was checking for his print and wasn't expecting to see the head of his dick hanging out of them. Markieff being Markieff didn't even try to hide it either. Serenity ran her tongue across her bottom lip admiring the meaty head.

"Yo, what you get me to eat?" Markieff asked, killing her thoughts.

"Huh?" Serenity said, snapping out of her fog.

"I asked you what you got me to eat?"

"Oh, some ranch wings and a salad.

"Bet. Let me wash my hands."

Markieff purposely left his tv on the playboy channel. For a second, Serenity sat there watching. She was getting aroused. Half of the shit they were doing she always wanted Aaron to do with her.

"I bet your sex life was whack with that nigga." Markieff said, coming back downstairs.

Serenity was so into what was in the tv, she never heard Markieff. It wasn't until Markieff walked up behind her pressing his hard dick against her ass. She jumped and turned around.

"See, you can't handle this shit." Markieff joked and sat down. He grabbed the remote and turned the channel. "Did you hear what I said?"

"When?" Serenity asked, sitting next to him.

"I said your sex life must have been whack. The way you watching it was like you wish it was you?"

"Boy, cut it out. I was just watching."

"Yea, ok," Markieff laughed. He grabbed his food and started to eat. "Yo, find something to watch. We can have a Netflix and chill type of night." Markieff suggested.

"I guess." Getting comfortable, Serenity kicked off her shoes and tucked her legs underneath her butt. Picking up the remote, she clicked on his Netflix and looked for something to watch.

"Aye, hit Luke Cage." Markieff told her.

Serenity hit the box for the show and laid the remote next to her.

"You still haven't heard from your boy?" Markieff asked, referring to Aaron.

"Check this. He lied about not being home for my birthday, so he could surprise me with a dinner and shit. It would have worked if I didn't know his dirty little secret. Apparently, his whack ass friends sent him a picture of us last night and this nigga had the nerves to say that makes us even. He admitted to cheating and accused me at the same time."

"Dude a fucking clown. Now that you know the truth, what are you going to do?" Markieff inquired, taking a bite of one of his wings.

Serenity shrugged her shoulders. "I don't know. I put his ass out and told him I needed some time to myself." Serenity paused and lowered her head, twirling her fingers. "Would I be stupid to go back?"

"Honestly, I'm not one to answer that. I mean with all the shit Shana did to me, I still went back. We can't help who we love." Markieff answered. "Let me ask you this, if you had somebody else on the sideline would you give him or her a chance"

Serenity busted out laughing. "Oh my God, I can't with you, I'm not bi."

"I didn't say you was, I'm just asking a question."

"No, because I shouldn't have anybody on the sideline."

Markieff nodded his head up and down. He finished his food and then got comfortable on the couch. He moved closer to Serenity and pulled her legs from under her and laid them across his. He then started rubbing her feet. It was something he used to do when they were younger. Serenity didn't know why but her heart started beating faster. Markieff looked at her warily.

"What's wrong?"

She shook her head. "Nothing."

Markieff didn't press the issue because he really didn't want to talk about her problems with Aaron. He had other things on his mind. He was a firm believer and knew if he and Serenity was meant to be, they would be. He was going to let things work out in their own way. He didn't want to pressure Serenity and make a decision and later regret it.

Getting even more comfortable, Markieff laid his head across Serenity's lap while he stretched his body across the couch. Not able to help herself, Serenity started playing with Markieff's ear. That was something else they did when they was young.

"Nah, you can't do that. That will get my homeboy down there going. Unless you willing…"

"Ok, I get your point." Serenity laughed. But ignored him and kept rubbing his ear.

It took every ounce of willpower for Markieff to behave. Unlike any other time, Markieff didn't get aroused. He closed his eyes enjoying the soothing feeling it was giving him. Not even twenty minutes later he was fast asleep. Serenity could hear her phone ringing in her bag and tried to move without waking Markieff up. Slowly, she lifted his head and laid it on the couch. When she got to her phone she rolled her eyes seeing it was Aaron texting, asking if he could come over to talk. She was glad she wasn't home at this point. Sitting back down, Markieff stirred around repositioning his body. He wrapped his arms around Serenity.

All she could do was laugh and lean back and watch tv with his six-foot-two, two-hundred-pound body draped across hers. Markieff tossed his body around and was now laying on his back. His hands then went down his pants causing Serenity to snicker.

"Why do men do that," she said out loud to herself.

It wasn't even seconds later Markieff's hands started moving up and down in his pants. Serenity's eyes grew wide seeing the size of his dick. She was so mesmerized by the thickness, it didn't dawn on her what was actually taking place. It was like she was watching Pornhub instead of Markieff jacking off.

SOUL Publications

"Fuck," Markieff moaned. His eyes was still closed and Serenity wasn't sure if he even realized what he was doing. But when she felt his hand grabbing hers, she had the answer to her question. "Just touch it Lucky."

It was like her hands had a mind of their own. They slowly made their way to his hard manhood. Leaning over she wrapped her hand around his thick dick and moved it up and down.

"Umm, just like that Lucky." Markieff wanted her bad and couldn't fight the temptation that was in front of him. He opened his eyes and looked up at her. "Lucky, I want your ass bad man." He hungrily glared into her eyes.

"Do you?" Serenity asked, challenging him to make a move.

Sitting up Markieff placed his hand on her leg. He leaned over and kissed her lips then went to her neck. His hands moved up her leg while he nibbled on her neck. He unbuttoned her pants and stuck his hand inside. She was soaking and wet as he played with her love button.

"You said you had something else for me to eat, can I taste it?"

"Yes," Serenity managed to say between panting heavily.

Standing to his feet Markieff pulled off his shirt. "Take off your pants and come lay over here," Markieff ordered, pointing to the long piece of the couch.

Once she was laying on her back, he positioned himself between her legs spreading them wider. He slipped his index finger inside of her and pulled it out. He looked into her eyes and saw something he already knew. She was begging him to get on with the shit. She wanted him just as bad as he wanted her. Licking his lips he lowered his head and kissed his way to her center. Taking his tongue he licked around her pussy lips before flicking it across her clit.

"Shiiittt," Serenity gripped the back of his head.

Feeling like she was dreaming Serenity couldn't believe what was happening. Markieff was sucking on her clit like a newborn baby sucks his mother's nipple for milk.

"Don't wake up, don't wake up," Serenity said out loud, feeling like she was dreaming and didn't want him to stop.

"What?" Markieff managed to say between slurps.

"Nothing. Don't stop, I'm about to cum," Serenity panted.

Markieff slipped his hands beneath her butt lifting it higher as he buried his face in her pussy. He looked up again with intensity in his eyes as he feasted on her sweet center. His tongue darted in and out of her pussy.

"I'm cuming," Serenity announced, trying to wiggle away.

Markieff gripped her hips holding her down firmly. He drilled his tongue deeper in her center. That alone sent her body into a surge of sensation. She came hard and even started to squirt. Markieff slurped up what he could. When he finally came up, his face was wet with her juices. Reaching for his shirt he cleaned his face. Hovering over Serenity a smile crept across his lips. Serenity was breathing heavily trying to recover from that mind blowing orgasm. Leaning forward, he kissed her neck

"We doing this?" Markieff asked for clarification.

Instead of using words, Serenity placed her hands on the back of Markieff's neck and pulled him in closer until their lips touched. She opened her legs wider for Markieff. He bent down and kissed her lips as he held his dick guiding it inside her awaiting center.

"Wait, you have on a condom?" Serenity questioned.

"For what? I don't have no STD. I wouldn't do that to you."

"Ok, I'm not on birth control. Since me and Aaron wasn't doing shit, I stopped taking them." Serenity informed him.

"And, I'm not a deadbeat daddy," he joked.

"Really," Serenity laughed.

"Shhh," he whispered as he continued his journey. Serenity gasped when she felt his thickness breaking in, but he quickly pulled out and yelled, "Fuck."

"What?" Serenity sat up.

"Girl, your shit dangerous. That shit so damn wet. Give me a minute shit." Markieff took his dick and rubbed it against her pussy lips, "Umm," he moaned closing his eyes.

"Stop playing and fuck me," Serenity begged.

Lifting one of her legs Markieff bent it at the knee sliding his hard flesh inside her. "Damn you feel so fucking good," he grunted thrusting hard and deep.

"Ohhhh you so deep, hold up," Serenity yelled, placing her hands on his chest.

"Nah, ain't no hold up. You told me to fuck you, right." Pushing deep inside Markieff growled with each thrust he delivered. "Damn Lucky." He couldn't believe how wet she was. He hasn't felt pussy like this in a long time.

"You hitting my spot. This dick feels so good," Serenity cried out.

"I know this." Markieff replied. So he wouldn't nut before he wanted to, he pulled out. Only putting the tip in, he pulled right back out and tip drilled her for a few seconds.

"Stop teasing and fuck me." Serenity cried out. She tried to wrap her legs around his waist to draw him in closer. Her pussy was throbbing, crying to have him back inside of her.

"Yo, you don't understand what's between your legs. Give me a second Ma. I'm not trying to bust early, shit."

Serenity covered her mouth trying not to laugh. This wasn't something she was used to because Aaron never did. He didn't care if he bust early.

"Turn over on your stomach." Markieff demanded.

Serenity did as she was told and Markieff positioned her like he wanted her. He rubbed his dick across her lips again, but this time Serenity wasn't patiently waiting. When she backed up on him his dick slipped right in. From there, she slammed her ass against his pelvis taking his thickness inch by inch.

"Ok, I see you, you trying to prove a point taking all this dick, I like that," Markieff smiled smacking her ass.

"Get it Kieff." Serenity purred.

Grabbing hold of her waist, Markieff took control again. He drilled her insides like she asked. He bullied her pussy and was loving the way her walls was squeezing his dick. Their bodies bumped harder against each other over and over.

"Get it Kieff, make this pussy cum again," Serenity coached.

"Stay still and let me get it then." Markieff rotated his hips in a circular motion before going in for the kill. He forcefully pounded her insides. He looked down and licked his lips seeing his dick glistening from her juices. He moved his hips in a steady motion feeling his nut coming back.

Serenity was at the peak of reaching her orgasm and started throwing her plump ass like she had something to prove.

"That's right Lucky, fuck this dick. Get that nut out for me." Markieff smacked her ass. "That's some good shit right here, fuck," he grunted again. He felt his load coming, but badly wanted to hold off. It was feeling too good and he didn't want it to stop.

"I'm cuming," Serenity yelled repeatedly.

"Fuck, me too baby."

Together they both released. Markieff pulled out and shot off his load on the floor. Once he was done he collapsed on the floor, still amazed at how good Serenity felt.

"Damn," he panted loudly.

Serenity climbed off the couch and collapsed on the floor next to him. Markieff pulled her closer to him and wrapped her up in his arms. She rested her head on his chest.

"Lucky, you know you got me on the sideline right? I'm not trying to pressure you into anything, but it's clear where your heart is." Markieff blurted out.

Serenity placed her finger over his lips. "Shh. Let's just savor this moment. I don't want to think about that stuff right now."

"Yea ok, but admit it, this shit felt right. You want it just as bad as..."

"Markieff."

"Ard."

Serenity couldn't believe how good Markieff made her feel. It was like he was making love and fucking her at the same time. He took his time with her and then fucked her like she needed to be fucked. Everything about Markieff just felt so right and it scared her. She knew what needed to be done.

***

"Lucky, wake up." Markieff shook her.

"Ugh, why?" Serenity grunted.

"Your phone going off. It could be Ki calling or something."

Serenity rolled her head to the side and looked over to Markieff. "What time is it?"

"Almost noon."

"Shit," she springs up. "I was supposed to meet Treasure for breakfast. She jumped off the couch and grabbed her phone out of her bag. She saw she had at least six missed calls. Of course, one was from Aaron. Two from Treasure and the other three was her mother. Treasure was the first call she returned.

"Girl, where are you? Your husband answered the door and was pissed because he thought you was with me. What the hell is going on here?"

"His ass shouldn't even be there. I'm sorry about breakfast. I stayed with Markieff last night and just getting up."

"Umm, he gave you that dope dick and put that ass to sleep. Yea, we will talk later. I will let you get back to that man. Call me when you get to your parents house."

Serenity couldn't help but laugh. "You are a mess but ok. Wait, are you still at my house?"

"Yep."

"Do me a favor and get me something to wear. I don't care what it is. I'm not coming over there if he's there. Just drop it off to my mother's house and I will change then."

"Ok boo."

Markieff tossed her a fresh pair of underwear and she looked up at him strangely.

"Boy, I'm not about to wear a pair of one of your jump off's panties."

"For your information, they don't belong to no damn jump off. I woke up and went to Walmart to get you a pack and a bra."

"Oh," was all she could muster up and say. "How did you know my size?"

"Umm, I know how to read the inside of a tag." Markieff laughed.

"Right."

"Go wash."

Serenity snatched the items she needed from Markieff and rolled her eyes. She got midway up the stairs and stopped. "Hey, you coming to join me?"

Markieff tucked his bottom lip. "Hell yea."

After their shower, they managed to get dress. Serenity put her clothes from the day before on and they headed over to her parent's house.

"Are we going to talk about what happened?" Markieff questioned.

"What is there to talk about?" Serenity shot back.

"Cut it out Serenity. Are you going to go back or are you going to look over at the sideline?"

Serenity knew she was touching his nerve because he called her by her name. She reached over and touched his hand. "Like you said, what's a title without the bond. Aaron and I lost that bond a long time ago. I'm ready to be loved."

Hearing her say that brought a big grin to Markieff's face. They arrived to her parents house walking hand and hand as they entered the house. They was so lost into each other, they didn't realize they was still holding hands or the fact that Aaron was standing there talking to Serenity's mother.

"Well, what do we have here?" Kathy asked with a big smile covering her face.

"Yea, what the fuck is this?" Aaron said getting loud.

Serenity snickered. "You don't have no room to ask questions. What are you doing here Aaron?"

"It's Sunday, I came to eat," he smirked.

"We not doing this. What part of I need time and space you didn't understand. That means my family is off limits too."

"My son is here. You're telling me I can't see him too?" Aaron questioned.

Kathy's eyes bounced from Serenity to Aaron then over to Markieff. "Umm, somebody care to explain what's going on?"

"Yea, you care to explain what's going on Aaron?" Serenity mocked, crossing her arms over her chest.

"Can we talk please?" Aaron pleaded.

"Oh, now you want to talk. I don't have shit to say to you. I told you when I was ready, I would. For now, can you please exit left and wait for me to make that call."

Aaron ran his hand over his head. "Yea, yea I guess. Can I at least take Kian with me?"

"Sure. Kian, come here," Serenity called out.

"Yes mommy?" Kian ran into the living room.

"You're going with your dad for a little. He needs to talk to you about a few things." Serenity said.

"Awe, man. I wanted to stay here with Unk and Kel." Kian whined.

"You can see them later. Right now, you need to go with your dad and I will see you later tonight." She kissed his forehead and watched as he pouted following behind Aaron.

"Serenity, what's going on?" Kathy questioned again.

"Aaron cheated," Serenity blurted out.

"Oh...ok. Say no more," Kathy laughed.

Serenity eyed Kathy warily. "Is that all you're going to say?"

"Markieff, can you give us a minute to talk?" Kathy asked.

"Sure. I need to holla at Mr. B and see what Kel doing."

Kathy walked over to her cabinet and grabbed two wine glasses. She then picked up her bottle of wine and waved for Serenity to follow her. They went out to the backyard and sat at the patio table. Kathy poured some wine into the glasses. Lifting hers she took a sip never taking her eyes from Serenity.

"What?" Serenity giggled.

"You know, when you were younger you always had this little glow. This certain kind of smile. As you got older that glow went away, and you rarely smiled that certain kind of smile. I take that back, you had that look when Kian was born. After that, I saw nothing. You then had this hard shell around you. Barely laughed and was always serious. I get it, but somewhere you lost yourself. All work and no play. If it wasn't about Kian, you didn't do anything. I told your father you got old at a young age. Today when you walked in that door I saw that glow, that certain smile and a little twinkle in your eyes." Kathy pointed out.

Serenity lowered her head trying to hide the fact that she was blushing.

"Umm hmm, I know," Kathy hummed. "Do you love him."

Serenity's head quickly popped up. "Huh?"

"If your black ass can huh, you can hear. You know what, let me rephrase that question. Are you in love him?"

Serenity started playing with her wedding ring. "Ma, I am. I been in love with Markieff since I was a little girl playing house. You couldn't tell me I wasn't going to be Mrs. Ervin," she chuckled thinking back.

"And so did he. He was young and scared of your father. Instead of acting on his feelings, he just kept you as a friend since Benny looked at him as a son. He felt like he was taking advantage of the opportunity because he was always here. He always had feelings for his bestie." Kathy informed her.

"And you know all this how?"

"Me and Markieff talked," Kathy smiled. "Baby, a man will constantly do what he thinks he can get away with. Aaron's actions was way louder than any words that could have been spoken. You was blinded and content with your situation, you didn't see it right away. I even saw you trying to fight for your marriage and Aaron still did him. Now that someone else has your attention, he wants to get some act right. I noticed he been home and at Sunday dinners. I can't tell you how to live your life. All I can do is make suggestions and I suggest you follow your heart." Kathy said, dropping some jewels on Serenity.

"Ma, can I ask you something?"

"Yes."

"Did daddy ever cheat?"

"He did. We was young and he was dumb."

"How was you able to forgive him?"

"Oh trust me, it wasn't easy. I didn't go back right away. You are the product of a make up baby," Kathy laughed. "I left your father for almost a year before I took him back. It wasn't until you was born we got married. So, don't look at our situation because it wasn't always good. We had our share of fights, ups and downs. The difference with our situation is your father is the one that fought for his relationship and it wasn't because some other man was trying to get with me. He realized what he had at home was worth fighting for on his own."

"I hear we got a problem to take care of," Benny snarled busting out the back door.

"No, we don't have no problem. Serenity is grown, and you sir are going to stay out of it." Kathy warned, giving him a stern glare.

"But..."

"Benjamin Beal, what did I just say?"

Benny squinted his eyes and threw his hands in the air. "Fine."

Kathy laughed and leaned over to Serenity. "See, I wear the pants in this marriage."

"Bullshit. Don't lie to that girl," Benny yelled, hearing Kathy.

Serenity picked up her glass taking a sip of her wine. Her mind was working overtime with so many thoughts. Looking into the house her eyes connected with Markieff who was standing in the kitchen. He winked at her causing her to blush again.

"Heyyy family," Shanita sung joining them in the backyard. "What y'all doing out here?"

"About to plan Serenity's divorce party." Kathy joked.

Serenity spit out most of the wine that was in her mouth and damn near choked on the rest. She coughed a little and yelled, "Ma," when she got herself together.

"What? I'm just keeping it real. You know you not staying with that jackass."

"Auntie you a mess." Shanita laughed.

"Let me go finish this damn dinner. I see Markieff's in my pots." Kathy said, going back into the house.

"Diva in the house," Treasure announced. "Hey Momma K," she hugged Kathy.

"Hey baby. Talk to your friend."

Treasure looked at Serenity warily as she went over to the patio table. "What she talking about?"

"Serenity thinking about leaving Aaron." Shanita answered before Serenity could.

"Shit, about damn time." Treasure snickered.

"Ren, are you really about to throw away your marriage?" Shanita questioned.

"Umm, that will be a hell yea. The fuck," Treasure answered before Serenity could.

Shanita turned to Treasure with a smug look plastered on her face. "Why should she? They been together far too long to give up now? Nobody perfect."

"And your point is? Aaron's black ass been cheating far too long and fucked up his marriage. Why the fuck the woman always gotta accept the disrespect and shit. Fuck out of here with that nut shit." Treasure angrily shot back.

Shanita sucked her teeth and stood to her feet. "Whatever. I'm going inside and help with dinner. Ren, don't be stupid and regret it later."

"You still standing here?" Treasure hissed.

Shanita stuck up her middle finger and made her way into the house.

"I don't like your damn cousin. It's something about her that don't sit too well with me."

"Cut it. She cool, just misunderstood." Serenity tried to sound convincing.

"Umm chick, what's up? You look different like..." Treasure paused as her mouth hung open. "You fucked him didn't you?"

"Shhh." Serenity got up and grabbed Treasure's hand. She then dragged her to the garage that was on the side of the house. Once inside she closed the door and turned on the light. Her lips curled into a smile.

"Spill it."

"No lie T, that shit was the best I ever had. Markieff damn sure made sure his neighbors knew his name if they didn't already."

"Yesss, that nigga got my girl glowing and shit."

"I feel so damn guilty and I don't know why. Aaron cheated and I'm sure his ass didn't give a damn about my feelings. So, I don't even know why I feel like this."

"Don't you dare stress yourself over this shit either. Ok yea, you're still married and all that other shit. But guess what, you won't be for long so what's wrong with getting the goods now." Treasure laughed, trying to lighten up the mood.

"Don't laugh, but that nigga made me squirt. And he lasted more than five minutes. He almost didn't because he said my pussy was dangerous since it was so wet."

"Umm girl, that pussy get a different kind of wet when you're in love. It's a whole different level of energy." Treasure explained.

"For some sick reason, I understand what you're saying."

"Of course you do. You know any relationship that begins with friendship before any true feelings was developed are always the best. Sometimes it takes for us to meet the wrong person to know that the right one always been there. Hey you know what they say, let something go and if it finds its way back, it's meant to be."

"Yea, that's true and all but me and Markieff parted ways because he moved."

"My point exactly. He found his way back and his ass is right on time."

Serenity started blushing again. It sure did feel right with Markieff. Treasure and Serenity talked a little more before going into the house to join the rest of the family for dinner. Coming out the garage Serenity spotted Shanita and Egypt in the backyard. She was about to go over to them. What she witnessed next shocked the hell out of her. Egypt raised her hand and came down hard, smacking the shit out of Shanita. She then read Egypt's lips when she said, you acting like I was the only one that made the mistake. He's to blame too.

"Nope, mind your business Serenity, you got too much going on yourself," she told herself.

During dinner you could tell it was tension between Shanita and Egypt. Serenity noticed they both was giving each other dirty looks. After dinner Markieff took Serenity back to his house so she could get her car. Markieff got out and walked around the car to open her door. He extended his hand and helped her out. He pulled her in and hugged her.

"You good?"

Serenity nodded her head, saying yes.

"Cool." Makieff kissed her lips. "I will call you later."

"Ok."

Serenity drove home with the biggest smile on her face. For a woman that just found out the truth about her husband, she was doing better than most in her situation. Stepping into the house, her phone started ringing. Taking it out she let out a frustrated breath of air.

"Yes Aaron," she answered irritably.

"We pulling up."

"Thanks for the courtesy call." With that, Serenity ended the call and turned around to open the door. She crossed her arms over her chest and stood in the doorway.

Aaron pulled into the driveway and Kian jumped out the car. He ran to the house and hugged Serenity before he jetted inside to his room. Serenity was about to close the door when Aaron called out to her.

"Hold up," Aaron yelled.

Aaron walked up the steps. "Can I come in? I need to get a few things."

Serenity clenched her jaws then held the door open for him to step in. Walking pass Aaron bent down and kissed her on the cheek. Serenity quickly wiped her face.

"Don't do that." Serenity scowled.

"Oh, so I can't kiss my wife?"

"Soon to be ex-wife," Serenity shot back.

Aaron laughed as he made his way upstairs. Serenity stayed downstairs while he gathered his things. Ten minutes later, Aaron came back down. He had a bag and a dozen of the roses he got Serenity for her birthday in his other hand. He placed them in front of her on the table and sat next to her.

"I'm sorry." Aaron tried to sound sincere.

Serenity stood up and went to the other side of the room. "You're only sorry you got caught."

"No, I'm sorry I hurt you." He sat there, gazing at her. For a second, he had Serenity's attention and she quickly turned away. "Ren, don't throw us away over this…"

"Kill that Aaron, you threw this away when you went out fucking other bitches."

"Ok you're right, but can you hear me out?"

"Hear what Aaron, your lies?" Serenity snarled.

"I will own up to my mistakes, but you pushed me to make them. You forgot to be a wife. You started working and it was like fuck me. I come home wanting to make love to my wife but you're always yelling you're too sleepy or got a damn headache because you been dealing with Kian all day. Don't make this all..."

"You're really about to blame me for this shit? You know what, you're a piece of work."

"I'm not blaming you. Just putting the facts out there. I love you but you made me feel like I didn't matter and we was just going with the flow," Aaron smoothly said, trying to run game on Serenity.

Serenity stood there and listened as he rambled on about how she pushed him away and into the bed of other women. He was talking so much bullshit, Serenity truly thought he believed himself. Serenity's phone rung interrupting Aaron's speech. Looking down, a shy smile covered Serenity's face.

"Is that him?" Aaron blurted out.

Serenity ignored him and answered her phone. "Hey you."

"You good? You didn't call, are you home yet?" Markieff questioned.

"Yes I'm home. Talking to Aaron."

"The fuck he doing there? You need me to come over?"

"No, I'm good. I will call you back, I'm about to send him on his way."

Aaron snickered. He eavesdropped on her call until she ended it. Serenity turned her back to him causing him to stand up. When Serenity turned around Aaron was right behind her wearing a scowl.

"You fucked him, didn't you?" Aaron questioned.

"I'm not doing this with you. It's time for you to go," Serenity informed him. She went to walk away, and Aaron grabbed her arm turning her to face him.

"Answer me," he said through gritted teeth. His nostrils were flaring with anger.

"Yes I fucked him, happy now," Serenity screamed.

"Cool. You know what, fuck you and that nigga." Aaron snatched his bag off the floor and headed for the door. He grabbed the knob and turned back around. "Ren, do you love him?" Aaron asked, never turning around.

"Aaron, I'm not answering that. Look, we need to figure out some type of arrangement for you and Kian. I will talk to a lawyer and start up the papers for…"

"You really doing this?" Aaron turned around. "You letting this nigga come in and fuck us up…"

"You did this! You fucked us up Aaron!" Serenity yelled.

Kian couldn't take the fussing anymore. He stood at the top of the stairs. "Ma, you ok?"

Serenity's eyes shot up. "Yes baby, I'm good."

"Dad, it's time for you to go." Kian demanded.

Aaron narrowed his eyes looking at Kian. "Excuse me? Who the fuck you think you talking to? I'm your fucking father and you better show me some damn respect." Aaron started moving for the stairs, but Serenity stepped in front of him blocking his path.

"Aaron, you need to leave. I will call you in a few days." Serenity told him.

Aaron kissed his teeth and walked away. He snatched his bag again and left out the house. He slammed the door so hard, the picture of them that was on the wall came crashing down. Serenity looked down at the picture and knew at that moment her family was no more.

Chapter 15

I t's been almost a month and Aaron felt like his life fell apart with one snap of a finger. Since his separation from Serenity he couldn't sleep, eat or think. It was even affecting his work performance. His boss gave him one project to close and he has yet to start on it. He truly had no interest in finishing. He already had his mind made up and was going to tell Mr. Peterson he couldn't get the person to close the deal. Walking into his office, he rolled his eyes seeing Egypt.

"I should fire your ass," he mumbled walking by her desk.

"What's stopping you? You don't have a reason to do it and you know Mr. Peterson won't let you," Egypt smirked.

"Yea, because you fucking his son. Nasty bitch."

"Wow, sounds like a whole lot of hate in your voice. You just mad my sister found somebody else that could fuck and love her better. I told your black ass my sister was going to have you in your feelings."

"Fuck you. I should tell her ass you was one of the reasons our marriage was broken up."

"You know what, do it because I'm sick of you holding that shit over my head. Matter fact, I will do it." Egypt scoffed.

"Do it, I don't even give a fuck. Fuck her and that punk ass nigga she is shacking up with."

"Aww, the baby sound big mad. You big mad Aaron?" Egypt teased.

Before Aaron could reply, the phone started ring. He walked away while Egypt took the call. Seconds later, she was calling Aaron.

Walking into his office, Aaron took out his cell phone. He noticed he had missed a call from Kian's school and quickly dialed it back.

"Hey, this is Aaron Porter returning a call."

"Yes, Mr. Porter. I'm the nurse at the school and I have Kian in my office. We tried calling your wife, but she hasn't picked up. When we didn't get a answer from you, we called his Uncle and he's on the way." The nurse explained.

"Ok. I will come get him. My brother works down the hall and I'm sure he was headed to my office to pass the news. Thanks for calling."

"No problem."

Aaron stood to his feet and headed to James' office. He knocked on the door and was shocked to see Mr. Peterson. "Good morning."

"Morning Aaron." They both spoke.

"Jay, you don't have to get Kian, I will go get him."

James brows raised. "What are you talking about, I wasn't going to get Kian."

"But the nurse said she called his Uncle..." Aaron paused. "Fuck," he ran his hand over his face. "I have to go get Kian, he's sick. I thought the nurse was talking about you but clearly it's Markieff she's calling his uncle."

"Perfect timing. You can go talk to Markieff about closing out this deal while you're at it. It's been long enough," Mr. Peterson said.

"Yea, I'm on it," Markieff lied.

"Jay, we will finish this conversation later," Mr. Peterson said before leaving out the office.

"What was that about?" Aaron asked.

"Nothing. Are you going to talk to Markieff about selling at least one of the properties? You know the hotel sits on historic land and could be major for us. Even that damn barbershop."

"I'm not kissing that muterfucker ass for this shit. I will tell Mr. Peterson I couldn't get him to move on the properties and try to find something else to close on."

"Aaron don't make this fucking personal. This is our jobs and money on the line."

"Nothing personal kid, just not about to give that man my business."

"Stupid," James shook his head.

"Whatever. Let me go get my son before that nigga get to the school."

"You're sad Aaron. I told you karma would visit your ass." James said.

Aaron didn't respond. He left out the office and headed to Kian's school. Soon as he pulled into the parking lot he spotted Markieff walking out with Kian in tow along with Mykel.

"This muterfucker wants my life so fucking bad." Aaron mumbled. Once he got closer, he called for Kian. "Ki, come on."

"I'm going with Uncle Kieff. I don't feel too good daddy." Kian told him.

"Nah, you're going with me." Aaron snarled. He went over and pulled Kian by his arm.

"Dad, that hurt. You're making my stomach hurt again." Kian cried out.

Markieff didn't want to have to get physical but he roughly pushed Aaron back. "Yo, all that is not called for. You had your chance to pick him up and didn't answer the phone. Serenity's handling business and wanted me to bring him home, so chill. Let's not do this in front of him."

"Ki come on, I will take you home." Aaron snarled.

"Mommy told me to go with..."

"I don't give a fuck what she said. You're coming with me now let's go."

Markieff was going to be the bigger person in this situation for the boys. "Ki, go ahead with your dad."

"I don't want to." Kian whined.

Aaron was getting sick of his family picking Markieff over him. "Ki, let's go, now!"

Kian cut his eyes at Aaron and walked over tothe car. He slammed the door once inside the car and pouted, showing his wasn't happy. Aaron ignored the sad look painted on Kian's face.

"Ki, what's wrong with you?" Aaron questioned.

"I want to go home. I don't feel good," Kian cried with tears falling from his eyes.

Kian was in pain and Aaron didn't even pay attention. He was too bothered by Markieff's presence to even realize his son was sitting next to him in pain. Clenching his jaws and not ever looking over at Kian, he gave in.

"Fine, I will take you home." Aaron wasn't in the mood to go back and forth was his twelve-year-old son.

Pulling up to the house he once called home, Aaron blew out a frustrated breath seeing Markieff standing on the porch, hugged up with Serenity. When she saw him, her face was frowned up shooting daggers with her eyes.

"Ki, get in the car so I can take you to the doctor," Serenity snarled. She walked up to Aaron and got in his face. "What is your problem? What was the point of taking Kian from Markieff if you were just going to bring him home? If you were thinking, a real father would had at least took him to the damn doctor."

"Yea, well since he's such a momma's boy, he cried for you so now you can take him. For the record, I am a real father. You just painted this picture for our son and got him thinking I'm the bad guy."

"Oh, you did that on your own." Serenity snickered.

"Lucky, we need to go. Ki in pain." Markieff yelled out.

"You need to get over yourself and grow the fuck up," Serenity pointed her finger in Aaron's face.

He smacked her hand down and pushed her. "Get the fuck out of my face with that shit."

Markieff had enough. He ran over and without talking, he punched Aaron square in his face. Aaron stumbled back but caught his balance. He swung his arms connecting his punch.

Markieff laughed it off. "You hit like a bitch."

Aaron screamed and like a linebacker he charged into Markieff, lifting him off the ground and body slamming him. Before Aaron could make his next move Markieff delivered a powerful uppercut getting Aaron off him. Markieff then stood to his feet and gave Aaron a few body shots to his midsection.

"Stand up and fight me like a real fucking man. Fight toe to toe bitch." Markieff snarled, jabbing at Aaron. His fist connected with Aaron's face twice. "Yea, can't handle a straight up fight," Markieff taunted, sending another blow to Aaron's face. Aaron's head snapped back with each punch.

Aaron finally stepped out of the way of Markieff's fast hands and threw a punch of his own. He missed terribly hitting nothing but air. Markieff took advantage and sent a jaw rocking punch to Aaron's jawline dropping him to the ground.

"Pussy," Markieff snarled, looking down at Aaron.

Markieff then noticed Serenity had left. He took one more look at Aaron and shook his head. Markieff got in his car and left Aaron sprawled out on the ground in pain. Taking out his phone he called Serenity to see which doctor she was taking Kian to.

Aaron winced from the pain as he stood to his feet.

"Aaron, that's you? You need me to call the police for you?" His old neighbor called over from his yard.

"For what? Your ass stood there the whole fucking time recording that shit. Should have thought about calling them then," Aaron snarled. He limped all the way to his car and slammed the door once he got in. Looking in his rearview mirror, he checked his face out. His eye was black and his nose looked slightly crooked. He touched it and quickly moved his hand from the pain. "Fuck," he cursed. His phone dinged and he looked down at it. He had a Facebook notification from a post somebody tagged him in. He clicked on it and it was a video. Soon as it started he gritted his teeth. He looked over to the neighbor's house.

"You real childish Rashun," Aaron yelled.

"Worldstar," Rashun laughed.

Aaron shook his head and pulled out of the driveway. He called into the office and informed them he was working from home for the rest of the day. When he walked into house Nene was sitting on her couch with her face buried into her phone. She looked up when she saw Aaron.

"Oh my God, are you ok?" She jumped up and went over to Aaron.

"Yea, I'm good." Aaron pushed her out the way and sat down. His phone was buzzing again he knew why. Taking out this phone he went to the post of the fight and removed the tag. "Go get me some ice for my face," Aaron ordered Nene.

"Ask me nicely," Nene told him.

"I'm not in the mood to play with you. Just go get the damn ice, damn."

"Don't be coming in here with that attitude because she pissed you off. I'm not the fucking one," Nene sneered. "Humph, I'm not Serenity. Nigga got me fucked up," she mumbled going into the kitchen.

Aaron chuckled and laid back on the couch. Nene had one thing right she wasn't Serenity, and to that think he was thinking about leaving her for Nene was now beyond him. He was learning that good old saying, the grass isn't greener on the other side. Nene only wanted to spend his money. She didn't cook, she barely cleaned and now that he was there, they barely had sex.

"Here," Nene said, throwing the bag of ice at him.

"Why you gotta be so fucking childish."

"Why was you fighting?" Nene answered with a question.

"The nigga disrespectful that's why."

"Umm, disrespectful or you still mad he fucking Serenity?"

SOUL Publications

Aaron sucked his teeth. "I don't care about all that no more. He can have her for all care."

"I can't fucking tell. You know when you said the shit was over between y'all, I just knew I had you, but I don't. You still want her."

"I don't. Fuck her. Why you stressing this shit. I'm with you ain't I? Don't work my nerves over this dumb shit."

"Whatever. I'm going out for a while." Nene grabbed her bag and headed to the door.

"Yo, where the fuck you going? I'm man down over here." Aaron cried out.

Nene snickered and walked out the door.

Aaron shook his head. His phone was going off and he saw it was Serenity. He ignored her call thinking she was calling to fuss about the fight between him and Markieff. He didn't feel like hearing it, so he hit decline and turned off his phone. He didn't want to be bothered with nobody right now.

****

"Ugh, he's not answering his damn phone," Serenity hissed. She tried dialing Aaron's number again, but this time it went straight to voicemail. "Really, now it's going straight to voicemail.

"Clown," Markieff shook his head in disgust. He walked up behind Serenity and placed his hands on her shoulders. "Don't let that man get to you. Kian is going to be alright." He bent down and kissed the side of her face.

Serenity turned around and wrapped her arms around his neck. "I love you. I swear you came at a time I really needed you. I know it seems so sudden but..."

Markieff placed his finger on her lips. "Shh. Nothing was sudden. This shit was meant to be." He winked.

Moments later, Treasure came rushing in with Lamont following behind her.

"Girl, I got here soon as I got your message." Treasure hugged Serenity.

"Thank you. Girl, I panicked a little but everything should be ok," Serenity informed her. Moments later,

Serenity's phone went off and she quickly answered thinking it was Aaron.

"Where the fuck are you?" Serenity snarled.

"Umm, I was calling to see if you wanted to grab something to eat. Did I do something wrong?" Shanita said, coming on the line.

"My bad cuz. I thought you was Aaron."

"Is everything ok?"

"No. Kian have to get surgery to remove his appendix. I been calling Aaron's dumbass and he hasn't answered my calls.

"Oh no, which hospital are you at, I'm on the way." Shanita said.

"Where at Penn."

"Ok, I'm not to far from there."

Serenity ended her call just as the doctor came back out.

"Mrs. Porter, we are about to take Kian up and prep for surgery. You saved your son's life getting him here when you did."

"Yea, he started throwing up and was burning up." Serenity said.

"Don't worry, we will take good care of him and have him back to normal in no time." The doctor smiled.

"Thank you." Serenity shook his hand.

The doctor went off to get the surgery started. Serenity let out a sigh of relief. Taking out her phone she called Aaron again and got the same results. Markieff hated the pained look on Serenity's face and knew just what she needed. He grabbed her hand and led her down the hall.

"Where are we going?" Serenity questioned.

"Stop asking questions." Markieff laughed. He went to the family restroom and looked around before he opened the door and pushed Serenity inside.

"Boy, are you crazy? We are not..."

Markieff kissed Serenity's lips shutting her up. He backed her up against the wall pinning her against it.

"Bae, we cant' do it here." Serenity moaned.

"I don't see you stopping me, so shut up and let me relieve some of that stress you got built up." Markieff started kissing on her neck as his hands unfastened her pants. He pulled them down and told her to step out of them while he freed himself from his sweatpants. Once his hard manhood was out he lifted Serenity up and eased her down on his length.

"Shhiitt," Serenity gasped.

"Yea, you need this." Markieff slowly stroked her insides getting her just right.

"Umm, just like that baby," Serenity panted, loving how Markieff took his time with her. He was teasing her spot making her beg for more. She wrapped her arms around his neck and pulled him in for a kiss.

Markieff picked up his pace bouncing her up and down as fast as he could.

"Get it from the back," Serenity begged.

A smile creased Markieff's lips. He put her down and with a smirk on her face, Serenity went over to the sink and bent over. Markieff tucked his bottom lip running his hand up and down his dick as he walked over to where Serenity was waiting. He beat his dick on her pussy before sliding back inside her wet, warm pussy.

"Fuck," Markieff grunted. He was still amazed about how good Serenity's pussy walls gripped his dick. He pulled out and then pushed back in with force going deep.

"Yes, just like that," Serenity praised him.

He gave her long, deep thrusts. He held onto her hips going fast, knowing this had to be a quickie. He lifted one of her legs placing it on the counter so he could go deeper. Serenity was now singing his name with each thrust he delivered. He hit her spot each time, waking up the beast in her. She started moving her ass meeting his every thrust.

"That's right, fuck me back." Markieff panted. He could feel his build up. His grip around her waist got tighter and he couldn't hold out like he wanted to. Serenity was reaching her peak because she picked up her pace and her walls was squeezing the life out of his dick. After a few more pumps Markieff was pulling out and jacked his dick as he let out his load.

They both cleaned up and Markieff cleaned up the mess he made on the floor. Serenity wiped herself and fixed her clothes. She then looked in the mirror and fixed her hair. She looked over to Markieff.

"You play too much, knowing this was not the place, but I needed that. Thank you, baby." She got on her tippy toes and kissed his lips.

"Anything for you."

When they got back to the waiting area Treasure gave them the side eye.

"Just nasty," Treasure teased.

Serenity's phone went off and it was Kathy calling. "Hey momma."

"Hey we just landed and got your message. Is Ki ok? Do we need to come back?"

"No, don't come back. Enjoy your trip. He will be fine." Serenity ensured her.

"You sure?" Kathy asked for clarification.

"Yes, I'm sure. You and daddy have a good time and we will see y'all when y'all get back. Love you."

"Love you too. Kiss Kian for us."

Serenity's phone hung up. She pulled it from her ear and saw her phone was completely dead. She didn't have her charger because she rushed out the house.

"Damn, my phone dead." Serenity sighed.

"Want me to run to the house and get your charger?" Markieff asked.

"Please," Serenity stuck out her lips.

"Cut that out," Markieff laughed. I will drop Mykel off too. "Mont, ride with me."

"I'm going to the café to get something to drink, you need anything?" Treasure asked.

Serenity shook her head. "No, I'm good."

Serenity took a seat in the chair and her leg started bouncing up and down. She was pissed Aaron wasn't even picking up the phone, knowing damn well Kian was sick. She picked up her phone to call Aaron again, but quickly remembered it was dead.

"Can I see your phone?" Serenity asked Shanita.

Not thinking, Shanita handed over her phone. Serenity thanked her and got up and walked across the room. She started keying in Aaron's number, but it was already programmed into Shanita's phone.

"What the fuck," she mumbled.

Instead of making the call, she went to Shanita's call history. Shanita made a call to Aaron not long ago. Treasure walked up and noticed Serenity's demeanor had changed.

"Ren, you ok?" Treasure asked out of concern.

"I don't know. I think I found out who Aaron's been fucking. I think it's Toni. That would explain why Shanita got his damn number saved in her phone. She called him probably trying to warn him and her slut ass friend.

Treasure chuckled. "Ren, don't be so damn naïve. It's her who's fucking Aaron. Did you check her text messages?"

"No, I didn't." Serenity said. She looked over to Shanita who was now looking at them warily.

Serenity turned back around and started scrolling through Shanita's phone. Serenity couldn't believe her eyes. Her heart rate started to race. It felt like the air in her lungs was sucked out, she couldn't breathe. How could two people that was supposed to care about her hurt her this way. She could hear Treasure asking what was wrong but blacked out. Not saying a word, she went over to Shanita and as powerfully as she could smashed her balled fist into her face. Shanita fell back on the chair and Serenity got on top of her beating away at her face.

"You bitch. All this time I was venting to you about Aaron, you been the one fucking him you bitch. You dirty bitch," Serenity yelled, sending blow after blow to Shanita's face.

"What the hell is going on. Why are you standing there letting Serenity and Nene fight like this?" Egypt asked, coming into the waiting area.

"What fight? Ren beating the hell out that girl and for good reasons. I knew y'all cousin was shady ass hell. The bitch been fucking Aaron." Treasure told her.

Minutes later, the security guards arrived and broke up the fight.

"You dirty bitch. I hate you. I fucking hate you. You fucked up my marriage." Serenity yelled.

"Get her out of here," the guard instructed his partner as he took Serenity down the hall. He remembered Serenity when she came in with Kian because he helped carry him in. The guard knew she needed to be there for him, so he was trying to save her from going to jail. "Ma'am, please chill out. If they call the cops, I have to tell them what happened. Your son needs you," he pleaded.

Serenity slowly started to calm down when the guard mentioned Kian. "Ok, I'm fine," she ensured him.

"You sure? I hate to put you out at a time like this."

"Yes, I'm good. Long as that bitch isn't here."

Markieff came around the corner. His car keys were in Serenity's bag so he came back to get them. That's when he saw the security guard with Serenity in the corner.

"Lucky, what the hell wrong with you? This wasn't the time or place for that. Kian needs you." He fussed.

"I know. I just blacked out." Serenity lowered her head.

"Did you at least win?" Markieff joked.

"Really," Serenity snickered.

The guard couldn't help but laugh himself.

"Scott, another fight broke out in the same area. I'm still with this chick and Dexter on the second floor. Can you get around there," the other guard yelled over the two radio.

"Yea, I'm going now," Scott the guard replied and took off.

Moments later, Serenity could hear Treasure's voice. She then took off and went to see what was going on. When she got to the waiting area she saw Lamont was restraining Treasure, and the guard was just standing in front of a crying Egypt who had a busted lip.

"What is going on here?" Serenity questioned, looking from Treasure to Egypt.

"Go ahead and tell her Egypt," Treasure yelled. "Tell her the real reason you and Shanita fell out."

Serenity's eyes locked on Egypt. "You...you knew them two was fucking and didn't say shit. You let me walk around this long, knowing that nigga been cheating on me and let me vent to your ass about it. You could have saved me the stress by telling me the truth."

"Nope, try again." Treasure scoffed. "See when you dropped miss thing's phone, I picked it up. So, you know my nosey ass went to reading messages and I came across one that was very enlightening. Not only was your trifling ass husband fucking your cousin, he was fucking your sister. So, I had to tag the bitch since you weren't around to do it."

The whole room gasped at the shocking bombshell Treasure just dropped. Serenity stood there blankly staring at Egypt feeling numb. She closed her eyes and visions of Egypt, Shanita and Aaron laughing at her raced into her mind. As much as she tried to keep her tears at bay, they came rolling from her eyes. She wanted to beat the shit out of Egypt but her feet wouldn't move.

Egypt stood there sobbing saying how sorry she was. She felt like shit and was embarrassed. She didn't want to see her sister hurt like this.

"I'm sorry. I never meant to hurt you," Egypt started to say.

"Bullshit. I read the messages. You only stopped fucking Aaron because you found out about Nene. You didn't care about your sister's feelings when you was fucking her husband."

Egypt looked around and saw all eyes was on her. Feeling defeated, she bolted out of the hospital.

"Damn, her ass got her Flo Jo on and got the fuck out of here," Lamont laughed.

"I'm sorry Ren, but you had to know. That secret been kept far too long." Treasure apologized.

Serenity went over to Treasure and hugged her. "Thank you."

"No thanks needed. You're my girl and I got your back."

For the next hour, they sat in the waiting area for the doctor to come out with an update. The guys went off to the café and Treasure looked over Serenity. She then got up and sat next to her, hugging her.

"How could they do me like this?" Serenity sobbed.

"Fuck them."

"I mean, my blood. My own blood betrayed me over dick." Serenity cried.

Moments later the doctor came over and told them Kian was out of surgery and was in a room. Markieff and Lamont returned as in time to go up to Kian room. Just as they were going to the room Aaron came rushing into the entrance door.

Not knowing what was going on Aaron grabbed Serenity stopping her. Instantly, everything went black and she smacked him hard across the face.

"Yo, what the fuck wrong with you?" Aaron questioned, holding his face.

Lamont stepped forward before either Markieff or Serenity could fuck him up. "Dude, I know your son is here, but right now is not the time for you to be here."

"Nigga, don't tell me where I need to be. I'm going to see my son so where is he?" Aaron snarled.

"Markieff, let's go," Serenity said, following behind the doctor, leaving Aaron standing there.

Aaron tried to step around Lamont and follow behind as well, but Lamont stepped in front of him.

"Umm, let me enlighten you. Your wife, I mean ex-wife just found out about your side chicks. Does, Nene and Egypt ring a bell?" Lamont taunted Aaron.

Aaron's mouth hung open. He ran his hands over his face, taking a step back.

"Yea, go home and maybe I can negotiate some type of visitation for you homie, but right now it's best you." Lamont informed him. "And judging from that video on Facebook, I don't think you want to get your ass beat again."

Aaron kissed his teeth. "I'm only going because I know emotions are running high. Tell Serenity to call me to let me know how Kian is doing."

"Oh, now you care about your son. She been calling you for hours and you didn't answer the phone." Treasure snarled.

"Bitch, mind your fucking business. Nobody..."

Before Aaron could finish, Lamont sent his fist crashing into his face. "Watch how you talk to my old lady. Only bitch in here is your ass. Now you can forget about me getting you visitation rights. Come on T," Lamont said, grabbing Treasure's hand.

Aaron grabbed his face and looked around. Everyone had their phones pointed at him. Taking his loss, he left out of the hospital.

Chapter 16

Aaron sat at the bar throwing back shots. Reality finally hit him. If he didn't think his marriage was over before, he did now. He let the strong taste of Henny burn the back of his throat. He looked up and saw that James and Calvin was walking into the bar. He was too stressed to hear their mouths but he had nowhere to go.

"Looks like that plan of yours didn't work out huh," James teased.

"Jay, I don't feel like hearing your shit." Aaron scoffed.

"Oh, you're going to hear it. Men like you kill me thinking they got everything handled, taking for granted what they got at home. How that shit playing out for you bruh?"

"Jay, fuck you ard."

"I think you done enough fucking," James joked. "I still don't understand why you got married. People get married because they loved that person they with and see them spending their lives together. Like I said, you should have left Serenity when you first got back with Nene."

"Jay, I said chill with the fucking sermon. I know what I did ard. I don't need you reminding me. Fuck," Aaron fussed.

"I know a good divorce attorney." Calvin said. "He helped my brother and..."

"I don't need no fucking attorney because I'm not getting no damn divorce. All my cards are on the table and now, me and Serenity can work out our problems," Aaron said, taking a sip of his drink.

"This fool done had too much to drink. Nigga, Serenity done moved on and you need to get that through your head."

"Well, if I can't have her, neither will he," Aaron slurred. He picked up his beer and James quickly took it.

"That's enough for you. You're in here talking out the side of your neck. You fucked up. Own up to that shit. You fucked up Serenity's life and she found somebody to pick up the pieces you broke. Be a fucking man and own up to your fuck ups. Cal I'm out man, I'm not about to sit here with this fool."

Aaron's phone buzzed and he had a text message from his neighbor telling him that Serenity tossed out all his shit onto the lawn. He tossed his phone not caring.

"I'm done here," Aaron stood to his feet. He took out his wallet grabbing a hundred dollar bill and tossed it on the counter. He went to his car and when he got in, he had to think about where he was going. With no destination in mind he just drove around. An hour later, he found himself parked outside the hospital. Not caring about anything, he got out and went inside. He went to the desk and found out which room Kian was in and headed upstairs. When he got to the door he could hear voices. He stopped and ear hustled the conversation.

"How you feeling Ki?" Aaron heard Markieff.

"Better. Where's my mom?"

"She went to the house to get some clothes. You have to stay for a few days."

"Man, I don't want to stay here," Kian whined.

"You will be ard." Markieff laughed.

"Unk, are you my mommy's boyfriend now?" Kian asked.

"No, we are just friends. Your mother is still married to your dad."

"But, I want her with you. She's happy when you're around and I like when you're around too. I mean you suck at Madden and 2k, but your cool and fun. My dad never played the game with me. He used to be fun, but he changed."

Aaron's jaws clenched hearing what Kian told Markieff. Not only did he lose his wife, he lost his son as well. His hate for Markieff was real and he wanted blood.

***

Across town, back at her house Serenity was packing her and Kian's clothes. Her mind was still on overload from all the secrets that was revealed. Never in a million years would she have thought her own sister would betray her. Shanita, she could see and really didn't care but Egypt her blood, was a hard one to stomach. Needing answers, she picked up her phone and called Egypt. She answered on the first ring.

"Serenity, I'm so sorry," Egypt cried into the phone.

"Why?" Serenity dryly asked.

"I have no explanation other than it just happened." Egypt honestly answered.

"Sad, just fucking sad. It just happened. Out of all the men running around Philly you had to fuck mine. Just know, it's on sight every time I see you."

"Don't worry, you won't see me for a while," Egypt said. I already called mommy and daddy and told them everything."

Serenity let out a chuckle. "Yea and how that conversation go?"

"Like I thought it would. Mommy told I was wrong in a nice nasty way and daddy flat out told me I was a disgrace. You always been his favorite, so this was excepted. Serenity, I'm truly sorry."

SOUL Publications

"No, don't do that. You will not sit here and try to play on my emotions. So, you think running will help you?"

"No, but it beats being looked down on and judged. Yes, I fucked up and I'm sorry. Darren already had plans to move to South Carolina, so I'm going with him."

"You know what, I should tell Darren to leave your bitch ass but I'm not even going to. Nobody else needs to be hate in this situation. I will pray for you." Serenity said, ending her call.

At this point, she didn't give a fuck about Egypt, Shanita or Aaron for that matter. She didn't even care to hear Shanita's poor excuse for fucking her husband. At the end of the day, she felt like she still came out on top. She had the man of dreams. Markieff was heaven sent and everything she needed to complete her life. Her phone rung and she smiled answering it.

"Yes sir?"

"Where are you?" Markieff asked.

"About to leave the house now. I had some stuff I had to throw out."

Markieff let out a snicker. "You tossed that man shit outside didn't you?"

"Well, yea," Serenity laughed.

"Crazy ass. Well, hurry back. Kian's up and asking for you."

"I'm on the way." Serenity looked around and something crossed her mind. "Hey, you know once I get this divorce finalized we need to go house hunting. I don't want to stay here. I want a new start with everything."

"Anything for you."

"Ok. See you soon."

****

Aaron took time off from work after his whole ordeal with Serenity. It's been two weeks and he was just returning to work. Soon as he got out his car an older white guy approached his car.

"Aaron Porter?" The guy asked.

"Yea, who's asking?"

Handing Aaron an envelope, he said, "You been served.

Aaron snatched the envelope. Walking into the building everyone was staring at him. He ignored the dirty looks and headed to his office. Opening the envelope Aaron's head was down, not paying attention to who was sitting at the front desk.

"Egypt, I need to see you in my office," Aaron said, never looking up.

"Sir, my name is Megan." The new assistant informed him.

Aaron's head quickly popped up. "Oh, Megan. Where is my assistant?"

"She resigned. You would have known this if you came to work. Meeting in the boardroom in ten minutes." James snarled.

"Whatever." Aaron went into his office finally taking out the papers. Not even reading the whole thing he tossed them on his desk.

"Mr. Porter, Mr. Peterson is waiting to see you in his office." Megan said over the intercom.

Aaron got up and walked down the long hall to Mr. Peterson's office. He knocked on the door and waited for him to answer.

"Come in," Mr. Peterson's voice boomed from the other side.

Aaron walked in not paying attention that someone other than Mr. Peterson was in the office.

"Aaron, I know you took some personal days off but you left when we had a big project on the line. Have you even tried to reach out to Mr. Ervin about the deal we had?"

Aaron cleared his throat and recited the lie he had planned to tell Mr. Peterson when asked this question. "See, I did reach out to him and just like my father in law, Mr. Ervin didn't want to sell. I even tried giving a higher price and he turned me down.

"Now why would you lie like that bruh. You never asked me shit." Markieff's deep voice boomed from the other side of the office.

Aaron's head quickly turned around to face Markieff.

"Sir, he's lying. Look me and this guy have some issues outside of work and I believe he is using that and making it personal."

"Aaron, let me stop you right there. I know about what's going on and Mr. Ervin assured me he never would mix his personal with business. And that's just why he sold us one of the hotels, thanks to James reaching out. Aaron, I'm sorry but because of this I'm letting you go. You allowed your feelings to get in the way of us making money."

"Right. There is no secret that I hate your ass, but I don't let shit mess up my money. Only reason Benny never sold you the property is because your punk ass thought he was supposed to hand it to you. You never showed him the numbers or anything to bait him. All you had to do was your job and shit could have happened." Markieff told him.

It felt like the room was spinning as Aaron stood there. He couldn't have heard Mr. Peterson right. "Sir, did you say you was letting me go?"

"Yes, you're fired. Have your things out the office by the end of the day." Mr. Peterson demanded

Aaron bit down on the folds of his cheek. He narrowed his eyes as he walked passed Markieff. Single handedly this man came in and fucked up Aaron's whole life. That was the last straw for him.

Markieff was going to pay for making his life a living hell. Aaron went to his office and grabbed everything that was important to him. He couldn't believe he was fired.

"Fuck this job," Aaron snarled out loud.

Once he had everything packed into the boxes he had, he left out the building not looking back. Taking out his phone he sent Serenity a text. He tossed his phone on the driver seat and sped off on a mission.

*****

"Bae, stop laughing. This is serious," Serenity fussed into the phone. She just informed Markieff of the text Aaron just sent her.

"I'm not worried about that man. Lucky, he just talking out the side of his neck. The man just got fired and angry. He a bluff. Nigga not going to kill me."

"Kieff, I don't know. Aaron does own a gun and..."

"I have one too and what." Markieff said irritated. "Don't worry, I will be ok. Aaron just in his feelings and trying to scare you. I will be fine."

"Ok. Just call me when you're on your way."

Serenity ended her call and tried calling Aaron to talk some sense into him. Serenity couldn't understand what he was mad for when he created all the problems he was facing. Going into the kitchen, Serenity went ahead and started dinner. Before she could reach the kitchen somebody was ringing her door bell.

"Girl, is that Aaron sitting across the street?" Treasure asked, peeping Aaron's car.

Serenity sucked her teeth. "Yea, that's him. Girl, hurry up and get in the house.

Moments later, Markieff pulled into the driveway. Next, Serenity saw Aaron getting out his car headed across the street. Raising his hand Aaron called out for Markieff to turn around.

"The fuck you want?" Markieff scoffed.

Not saying a word, Aaron pulled the trigger sending three shots towards Markieff, dropping him to his knees. Instantly, Markieff started gasping for air falling to ground.

"No, no, no," Serenity cried out, rushing over to Markieff. She cradled his head in her lap and rocked back and forth. "Don't you die, please don't die."

Blood was pouring out of Markieff's body and he was fighting to keep his eyes open.

"I...I love you Lucky. I had plans to marry you soon as your divorce was done. Now, I guess that's not happening." Markieff slurred.

"No, don't talk like that. You're going to make it." Serenity cried.

"I called 9-1-1 they sending somebody." Treasure informed her.

Serenity looked up and was surprised to see Aaron still standing there with the gun in his hand. His eyes was dark and in front of her wasn't the man she once knew. Aaron's eyes was filled with hate and Serenity didn't see any type of remorse for his actions. Looking back down, Serenity rubbed the side of Markieff's face.

"I... I always loved you," Markieff confessed before fading to black.

The Letter

One year later...

"Ma we going to be late, come on," Kian fussed, trying to rush Serenity.

"Boy, don't be rushing me I'm coming."

They were headed to her parent's anniversary party and she was moving a bit slower than usual. She went over to her full length mirror and did a once over, making sure she was looking good.

"Ugh, I'm fat," she mumbled.

"Ma, it's six." Kian fussed again.

"I'm coming boy." Serenity grabbed her bag and phone and took her time going down the steps in her heels.

Kian shook his head. "About time."

"You look pretty Mama Luck," Mykel smiled.

"Thank you Kel." Serenity stuck her tongue out at Kian. "I'm glad you're hanging with us this week Kel. We missed you."

"Yea, I missed y'all too. I wish my dad was here." Mykel sorrowfully said.

"Me too." Serenity half smiled.

"Me Three," Kian added.

They all left out the house and headed to the hall where the party was held. Pulling up Serenity smiled, happy to see so many people there to celebrate with her parents. Just as she pulled up Treasure and Lamont was walking to the front door.

"Ayee, there goes my girl." Treasure smiled.

"Girl, come help me. My legs been hurting me and I can't get out this damn truck without jumping down."

"Ugh, come on fat girl," Treasure teased.

The Dj was playing some old school music and everyone was on the dance floor having a good time. Kathy spotted Serenity and came over to her hugging her.

"Thank you baby, for throwing this party."

"You're welcome."

"Oh, I got something for you." Kathy walked off and went over to her table. She grabbed something from her bag and walked it back to Serenity. "This came for you today."

Serenity read the envelope and her heart dropped to her feet. "Ma, I will be back," she said, walking off. As she went to the back of the hall, she ripped open the envelope and took out the paper that was inside. She unfolded it and started reading.

Dear Serenity,

I must have written this letter a million times but never had the courage to send it off. Before I met you I was with Shanita. I had just moved to Philly and met her. We hit it off and started dating. I fell for her but found out she was with someone else. We broke up and that was that. I met you not knowing she was your cousin. It wasn't until the wedding I knew. She said not to tell you about us and like a fool I agreed. A few years later, I bumped into her in Vegas. She was a flight attendant. We went out for drinks and started reminiscing about the old times we had. One thing led to the next and we crossed the lines of no return. As far as things with Egypt, I can't even remember how we got there. One night we was at work and she was venting about Darren. I called myself trying to comfort her. She kissed me and I allowed temptation to control me.

I know saying sorry can't make up for the pain I caused you and Kian, but I'm truly sorry for what I done. I wasn't thinking about what my selfishness would do to the people around me. It tore my family apart and ruined the lives of others. I wish I could turn back the hands of time. I would do everything right. Talking to this old head in here helped me see that I took you for granted, and I know now that I did. The one thing I didn't think about when I was out cheating was the fact that I could lose you. Furthermore, I didn't think I would lose you to the hands of another man. I became bitter and didn't know how to handle what I dished out to you. I pray one day you could forgive me and maybe bring Kian to see me. If not, I will wait until my ten year sentence is over. It's not much I can say because I know I'm the last person on earth you want to hear from. I hope all is well with you and I know you're taking good care of my son. Take care Serenity. Love, Aaron.

Serenity let out a sigh of relief getting the closure she needed. Although she was over that past life, she was glad for the answers to the questions that was in the back of her mind. She balled the paper up and threw it in the trash can in front of her. She missed and had to go over and pick it up. When she bent down she felt someone behind her.

"Girl, don't be bending over like that," Markieff said, wrapping his arms around her.

"Oh, I hate you. You said you wasn't going to make it home in time for the party." She turned and playfully hit him.

"I didn't think I would because my flight was delayed. What you doing back here?" He bent down and kissed her lips.

Serenity let out a sigh. "Aaron sent me a letter to my mother's house. I came back here to read it."

Markieff touched her shoulder and sucked his teeth. "Fuck that nigga. He lucky his ass got booked. I swear, I'm glad his ass didn't have no damn aim. I thought for sure I was done."

"That was the scariest day of my life."

"Me too."

Serenity felt a sharp pain in her stomach and grabbed it.

"What's wrong?"

"Your daughter in here kicking me like she crazy."

Markieff laughed and placed his hand on Serenity's belly. "Tell mommy you're not crazy. You heard daddy and got excited. I can't wait to meet you baby girl," he rubbed her belly.

"Me too," Serenity smiled.

"I love you, soon to be Mrs. Ervin."

"I love you more, Mr. Corny ass Ervin."

Treasure and Lamont came strolling to the back for their own personal reasons when they saw Markieff and Serenity.

"Ugh, do you two ever take a break from fucking." Lamont said.

"Looks who's talking," Markieff shot back.

"See, we came back here to get you two. They ready to cut the cake," Lamont lied.

"Umm hmm," Serenity hummed.

They all burst out into laughter. Serenity couldn't help but smile. The past year had been hard for her, but she overcame all the obstacles. She hated she had to lose a few friends along the way, but that's how life works. Aaron was now serving a ten-year prison sentence for attempted murder on Markieff. They said it was a crime of passion and gave him the minimum sentence. But it wasn't all bad for her. Her divorce was finalized, she and Markieff was due to get married and was expecting their baby girl in a month. She hasn't heard from or seen Egypt since she moved, and she was cool with that. She saw Shanita a few times and that was about it.

Life for Serenity was great and she couldn't ask for a better one. Markieff coming back was perfect timing and she thanked God every day for sending him when she needed him the most...

SOUL Publications